科學怪人

Frankenstein

原著 _ Mary Shelley

改寫 _ David A. Hill

譯者 _ 盧相如

ABOUT THIS BOOK

For the Student

🎧 Listen to the story and do some activities on your Audio CD.

▷◁ Talk about the story.

⭐ Prepare for Cambridge English: Preliminary (PET) for schools.

For the Teacher

HELBLING e-ZONE THE EDUCATIONAL PLATFORM A state-of-the-art interactive learning environment with 1000s of free online self-correcting activities for your chosen readers.

Go to our Readers Resource site for information on using readers and downloadable Resource Sheets, photocopiable Worksheets, and Tapescripts. www.helblingreaders.com

For lots of great ideas on using Graded Readers consult Reading Matters, the Teacher's Guide to using Helbling Readers.

Level 5 Structures

Modal verb would	Non-defining relative clauses
I'd love to . . .	Present perfect continuous
Future continuous	Used to / would
Present perfect future	Used to / used to doing
Reported speech / verbs / questions	Second conditional
Past perfect	Expressing wishes and regrets
Defining relative clauses	

Structures from lower levels are also included.

CONTENTS

Mary Wollstonecraft Shelley was born Mary Godwin in 1797. She was an English writer and wrote novels, short stories, plays and travel books. *Frankenstein*, published anonymously[1] in 1818 when she was 20, is her best-known work. She was married to the English Romantic[2] poet Percy Bysshe Shelley.

Mary's mother died when Mary was only eleven days old. Her father married his neighbor, Mary Jane Clairmont, four years later. In 1814, Mary Godwin fell in love with Shelley, who was married. Together with Mary's stepsister, Claire Clairmont, they left for France and traveled around Europe. They married in 1816 after the suicide[3] of Shelley's first wife, Harriet.

In 1816, Mary and Percy spent their summer holiday with Lord Byron and other friends near Geneva, Switzerland. This was where Mary began writing *Frankenstein*, after the friends had a competition[4] for the best horror story. The Shelleys left Britain in 1818 for Italy. They had two children but both of them died. Finally Mary had a son, Percy.

But in 1822, her husband died. His boat sank during a storm and he drowned[5]. A year later, Mary returned to England. She looked after her son and earned money as a writer. She was ill for the last ten years of her life. She finally died of[6] a brain tumor[7] at the age of 53.

Until the 1970s, Mary Shelley was known mainly for *Frankenstein*. But recently her other historical novels *Valperga* (1823) and travel books *Rambles*[8] *in Germany and Italy* (1844) were discovered.

---

1 anonymously [əˈnɑnəməslɪ] (adv.) 不具名地
2 Romantic [roˈmæntɪk] (a.) 十八世紀英國浪漫主義文學潮流（的）
3 suicide [ˈsuəˌsaɪd] (n.) 自殺
4 competition [ˌkɑmpəˈtɪʃən] (n.) 比賽
5 drown [draʊn] (v.) 溺斃
6 die of 死於（某疾病）
7 tumor [ˈtjumɚ] (n.) 腫瘤
8 ramble [ˈræmbl] (v.) 閒逛；漫步

ABOUT THE BOOK

Frankenstein is a novel about a young science student who creates a creature as a scientific experiment. It is a great horror story but also discusses ideas about philosophy and questions man's right to "play God[1]." It is a very early example of science fiction[2].

During the summer of 1816, Mary Shelley traveled to Geneva with her husband Percy Shelley, Lord Byron, and others. The weather was too bad for outdoor activities, so the friends spent time inside. They read ghost stories and then had a competition to write the best horror story. Mary dreamt about a scientist who created life but was horrified by the "thing" he had made; her dream became the story of *Frankenstein*.

As well as being a warning about the dangers of obsession[3], the novel also talks about the problem of being lonely. The monster only becomes violent because he is rejected[4] for his appearance, not because he is naturally evil[5]. He shows himself to have a good character[6] several times in his story.

When the book came out one critic[7] said it was "horrible and disgusting." Others were shocked that a woman had written it. But *Frankenstein* was extremely popular. It became widely known when it was made into a stage play in 1823. It has inspired[8] many films, TV adaptations[9] and plays since then.

1　play God 扮演上帝
2　science fiction 科幻小説；
　　科幻作品（= Sci-Fi）
3　obsession [əb`sɛʃən] (n.) 著迷
4　reject [rɪ`dʒɛkt] (v.) 拒絕

5　evil [`ivḷ] (a.) 邪惡的
6　character [`kærɪktə] (n.) 個性
7　critic [`krɪtɪk] (n.) 評論家
8　inspire [ɪn`spaɪr] (v.) 賦予靈感
9　adaptation [ˌædæp`teʃən] (n.) 改編

1 What do you know about the novel *Frankenstein*?
Tick (✓) true (T) or false (F).

- T F (a) The novel is a horror story.
- T F (b) Frankenstein is the name of the monster.
- T F (c) The author was a woman.
- T F (d) The story has a happy ending.
- T F (e) Part of the story takes place at the North Pole.

2 Match the sentences to the characters. Then listen and check.

Victor Frankenstein

The monster

Elizabeth

Henry Clerval

Robert Walton

William Frankenstein

- (a) A science student who creates a monster as an experiment.
- (b) An explorer who travels to the North Pole on a ship.
- (c) A girl who grows up with Victor Frankenstein's family.
- (d) A boy who has blond hair and blue eyes.
- (e) A very large man, who has superhuman powers.
- (f) Victor Frankenstein's good friend, who loves anything medieval, especially King Arthur.

3 Look at the picture of Frankenstein and his monster. Read the passage and then answer the questions.

Finally, one dark November night I completed my work. I collected my instruments and gave life to the being that lay at my feet. By the light of the candle, I saw the eyes of the creature open; it breathed hard; then made quick movements of its legs and arms.

How can I describe my emotions when I saw this disaster that with such endless work and care I had tried to create? I had selected his features as beautiful. Beautiful? Great God! His yellow skin only just covered the muscles and veins beneath; he had shiny black hair; his teeth were pearly white. But these good features only made a more unpleasant contrast with his watery eyes, lined face and straight black lips.

[a] When did Frankenstein complete his work?
[b] What color was the creature's skin?
[c] Did Frankenstein think the monster was beautiful?
[d] What were the monster's good features?
[e] What were his bad features?
[f] Find the words in the text that mean the following.

[1] tools _____   [3] feelings _____

[2] wrinkled _____   [4] chosen _____

[g] Which of these words does Frankenstein NOT use to describe his creation here? Tick (✓).
☐ being   ☐ creature
☐ disaster   ☐ monster

◁[4] Look at the names of some of the places mentioned in the story. Discuss with a partner what you know about them. Then look at a world map to see where they are.

North Pole Russia Geneva Ingolstadt London
Perth (Scotland) Orkneys Naples Ireland

[5] Frankenstein gets his parts for the monster from three places. Match the places below with their definitions.

1. a room where dead bodies are cut up for scientific study
2. a place where dead people are buried
3. a place where animals are killed

_____ a cemetery
_____ b slaughterhouse
_____ c dissecting room

[6] Complete the sentences with the correct word from Exercise [5].

a Frankenstein found body parts for the monster in the
_____ at his university.

b He found animal body parts for the monster at the
_____ .

c After he died, Frankenstein's brother
was buried in the _____
in Geneva.

7 Write the correct words of each sentence, using the words in the box below.

> tombs philosophy professors veins physiology
> anatomy chemistry decay muscles students

[a] Two kinds of people you would find at a university.

_____

[b] Four names of subjects studied at university.

_____

[c] Two words for parts of the body.

_____

[d] One word for small buildings where the dead are buried.

_____

[e] One word that means breaking down or becoming only bones.

_____

8 Choose the best word to complete the sentences.

[a] Mr Waldman, the chemistry professor, said that I should study natural _____ and mathematics.
 ① muscles   ② philosophy   ③ tombs

[b] After that, natural philosophy and _____ were my only occupation.
 ① muscles   ② professors   ③ chemistry

[c] My main interest was the living body. I studied physiology and _____.
 ① decay   ② tombs   ③ anatomy

[d] I spent days and nights in _____, watching the decay of human bodies.
 ① chemistry   ② physiology   ③ tombs

[e] The preparation of a body with all its muscles and _____ was extremely difficult.
 ① students   ② philosophy   ③ veins

Introduction

In the year 17—, an explorer[1], Robert Walton, traveled from England to Russia to find a way across the North Pole and into the Pacific Ocean. He wanted to be the first person to travel there by ship. He had been on many dangerous voyages[2], and studied mathematics, science and medicine. Walton often wrote letters to his sister in England to tell her about his travels. In one particular letter he told her a strange and terrifying story full of horror, agony[3] and anguish[4].

1 explorer [ɪkˋsplorɚ] (n.) 探險家
2 voyage [ˋvɔɪɪdʒ] (n.) 航海
3 agony [ˋægənɪ] (n.) 極度痛苦；苦惱
4 anguish [ˋæŋgwɪʃ] (n.) 極度的痛苦

August 5th, 17—

My dear sister,

Something strange happened to us this week. Our ship was surrounded[1] by ice and a thick fog. When the fog lifted[2], in the distance we saw a very large man on a sledge[3] pulled by dogs. He was traveling away from us. This was amazing because we were several hundred kilometers from land and other civilization[4].

The next morning the ice broke up, and while the sailors were getting ready to sail, they saw another man on a piece of ice! The man was frozen[5], thin and very tired. We immediately invited him to join our ship, but he said he first wanted to know where the ship was going. We told him we were going to the North Pole and he agreed to join us.

He said he was following someone who had run away from him. I told him about the very large man we had seen the day before. He became excited and asked me lots of questions. Then he told me his story, as a warning[6] to me and to all men. So now, dear sister, I will tell you the story that the man told me.

Chapter 1

My name is Victor Frankenstein and I am from Geneva. My father was a rich businessman and well-known in Switzerland. He married a poor woman, much younger than him. They traveled around Europe a lot and I was born in Naples.

My mother often visited poor people to help them. Once, near Lake Como, she visited a family with five hungry children. One little girl was slim and fair, different from the others. When my mother asked about her, the woman of the house said she was an orphan[7] and that her parents had been rich.

My parents agreed to take her and bring her up with their own family. The girl's name was Elizabeth, and she became my best friend. She was interested in poetry and nature, while I studied the physical[8] secrets of the world and how things worked. On the birth of my youngest brother, when I was seven, my parents stopped traveling and returned to Geneva, living in our town house and a country house by the lake.

---

1 surround [sə`raund] (v.) 圍繞
2 lift [lɪft] (v.) （雲、霧等）消散
3 sledge [slɛdʒ] (n.) 雪橇

4 civilization [ˌsɪvḷə`zeʃən] (n.) 文明世界
5 frozen [`frozṇ] (a.) 冰凍的
6 warning [`wɔrnɪŋ] (n.) 警告；告誡
7 orphan [`ɔrfən] (n.) 孤兒
8 physical [`fɪzɪkḷ] (a.) 自然界的

My other close friend was Henry Clerval, the son of a merchant[1]. Henry loved anything medieval[2], especially King Arthur and his knights. He often tried to make us act plays and become characters from the medieval world of chivalry[3]. Henry was interested in morals[4] and heroes and he wanted to become one when he grew up. We had a happy childhood. Elizabeth was good and kind and she watched over us with her soft smile and beautiful eyes.

Despite my happy and carefree[5] childhood I was always eager[6] to learn about other things. It was the secrets of heaven and earth that I wanted to learn about. When I was thirteen I found a volume of the works of Cornelius Agrippa[7]. This opened up a whole new world for me and I was very happy.

AGRIPPA

- Use the Internet to find out more about Cornelius Agrippa. Discuss your findings in small groups.

HENRICI COR-

NELII AGRIPPAE

VERA EFFIGIES

---

1 merchant [ˋmɝtʃənt] (n.) 商人
2 medieval [ˌmɪdrˋivəl] (a.) 中世紀的
3 chivalry [ˋʃɪvlrɪ] (n.) （總稱）騎士
4 moral [ˋmɔrəl] (n.) 道德

5 carefree [ˋkɛrˌfri] (a.) 無憂無慮的
6 eager [ˋigɚ] (a.) 渴望的
7 Cornelius Agrippa 阿格里帕（1486–1535）文藝復興時期的神祕學家

My father told me not to waste my time reading such books and did not explain anything to me. So I read on alone, following what I read from a child's point of view, not properly[1] understanding but still curious to learn.

This continued until a few years later when I saw the effects of a thunderstorm. A flash of lightning had completely destroyed[2] a tree and a learned[3] guest staying with our family told us all about a theory[4] he had formed on the subject[5] of electricity[6] and galvanism[7]. These subjects were new and interesting for me and, pushing my years of studying Agrippa to one side, I immediately threw myself into[8] the study of mathematics and science.

This was perhaps the last time that my "guardian angel[9]" tried to protect me from the storm that even then was waiting to fall on me.

---

1 properly [ˈprɑpəlɪ] (adv.) 正確地
2 destroy [dɪˈstrɔɪ] (v.) 毀壞
3 learned [ˈlɜ˞nɪd] (a.) 博學的
4 theory [ˈθiərɪ] (n.) 學説；理論
5 subject [ˈsʌbdʒɪkt] (n.) 學科

6 electricity [ˌilɛkˈtrɪsətɪ] (n.) 電學
7 galvanism [ˈgælvə͵nɪzm̩] (n.) 直電流
8 throw oneself into 投身於
　 (throw 三態：throw; threw; thrown)
9 guardian angel 守護天使；保護神

Chapter 2

At seventeen, the first misfortune[10] of my life happened. Elizabeth caught scarlet fever[11], and my mother looked after her. Soon, Elizabeth was cured, but my mother caught a terrible form of the illness and died. On her deathbed, she said that she hoped Elizabeth and I would marry.

I then left Geneva for the University of Ingolstadt. I was alone for the first time. My life had been extremely limited, and as I traveled, I thought with pleasure about the new knowledge that was waiting for me.

I immediately went to visit the main professors. Chance—or rather the Angel of Destruction, who was now in charge of[12] my life—led me first to Mr Krempe, professor of natural philosophy[13]. He was horrified that I had studied old writers like Cornelius Agrippa. He said I had completely wasted my time; then he wrote down a list of recent books that I should buy and read. However, I decided not to go to his lectures[14] because Mr Krempe was an ugly, short, fat man with an unpleasant[15] voice.

---

10 misfortune [mɪsˈfɔrtʃən] (n.) 災難
11 scarlet fever 猩紅熱
12 in charge of 接管
13 natural philosophy 自然科學（特別是物理學）
14 lecture [ˈlɛktʃə] (n.) 授課
15 unpleasant [ʌnˈplɛznt] (a.) 令人不愉快的

TEACHERS

- What are your teachers like?
- Tell a friend who is your worst teacher and why.
- Do you think it is important for your teacher to be nice or good at teaching? Discuss in small groups.

I then went to see Mr Waldman, the chemistry professor. He was very different: about 50 years old, with a kind expression[1] and a very sweet voice. His first lecture began with a history of chemistry, and recent developments. He then described the current state of the sciences, and explained many basic terms[2].

He also did a few experiments, and then said: "The ancient teachers of science promised impossibilities and performed nothing. The modern masters promise very little, but they have indeed performed miracles[3]. They have got new and almost unlimited powers."

As he said this, I felt truly alive. His words touched the center of my being, and soon my mind was filled with one thought: so much has been done, but I, Frankenstein, will do more. I will find new ways, explore unknown powers and open the world to the deepest mysteries of creation.

I returned to my old studies and devoted myself to[4] a science for which I believed I had a natural talent[5]. When I visited Mr Waldman and told him about my earlier studies, he said that I should also study natural philosophy and mathematics, as every chemist needed that knowledge. He also gave me a list of books to buy. This was a memorable[6] day which decided my future destiny[7].

---

1 expression [ɪkˈsprɛʃən] (n.) 表情
2 term [tɝm] (n.) 術語
3 miracle [ˈmɪrəkl] (n.) 奇蹟
4 devote oneself to 致力於；獻身於
5 talent [ˈtælənt] (n.) 天賦
6 memorable [ˈmɛmərəbl] (a.) 難忘的
7 destiny [ˈdɛstənɪ] (n.) 命運；天命

(10) After that, natural philosophy and chemistry were my only occupation[1]. I read the books and attended[2] the lectures. My progress was quick, surprising the other students and my professors. After two years of continual study and experiment, I made improvements in some chemical instruments[3] which brought me great respect at the university.

I had by then reached a point where the University of Ingolstadt could no longer help my development. I was planning to return to Geneva when something happened which made me stay longer.

My main interest was the living body. Where did life come from? It was a big mystery. I studied physiology and anatomy[4]. I spent days and nights in tombs watching the decay[5] of human bodies. And then after days and nights of work, I discovered the cause of life, and, more importantly, I became able to create movement in lifeless matter[6].

I thought about how to use this amazing[7] power. For, although I could give life, the preparation of a body to receive it, with all its muscles and veins[8], was extremely difficult.

Eventually[9], I decided to make my own creation. It would be two and a half meters tall and also broad, because the small size of much of the body created difficulties. After some months of collecting and arranging my materials, I began.

I was filled with enthusiasm[10] and energy. I could break through the knowledge of life and death and bring light into our dark world. I wanted to produce a new species[11] that would bless me as its creator. I hoped that in time[12] I would be able to bring back life after death. I worked day and night, I grew thin and pale. I collected bones from the cemetery[13], and the dissecting[14] room and slaughterhouse[15] provided other parts I needed. I worked in a separate room at the top of the house. At times I hated what I was doing, but a wild passion[16] made me continue.

---

1 occupation [ˌɑkjəˈpeʃən] (n.) 工作；專注
2 attend [əˈtɛnd] (v.) 出席
3 instrument [ˈɪnstrəmənt] (n.) 儀器
4 anatomy [əˈnætəmɪ] (n.) 解剖學
5 decay [dɪˈke] (n.) 腐朽
6 matter [ˈmætɚ] (n.) 物質
7 amazing [əˈmezɪŋ] (a.) 驚人的
8 vein [ven] (n.) 血管

9 eventually [ɪˈvɛntʃuəlɪ] (adv.) 最後地
10 enthusiasm [ɪnˈθjuzɪˌæzəm] (n.) 熱情
11 species [ˈspiʃiz] (n.) 種類；物種
12 in time 及時
13 cemetery [ˈsɛməˌtɛrɪ] (n.) 公墓；墓地
14 dissecting [dɪˈsɛktɪŋ] (a.) 解剖的
15 slaughterhouse [ˈslɔtɚˌhaus] (n.) 屠殺場
16 passion [ˈpæʃən] (n.) 熱情

In all this time I had no contact with my family. I never noticed the passing seasons. I kept away from fellow students. I slept badly and was often nervous and afraid, but still my purpose[1] burned in my mind like a bright light leading me on.

PURPOSE

- Have you ever had a purpose or project that kept you awake until you finished it? Something like a book you were reading, a project for school, a video you were making or a game you were playing? How did it make you feel? Tell a friend.

1 purpose ['pɝpəs] (n.) 目的
2 being ['biɪŋ] (n.) 生物
3 emotion [ɪ'moʃən] (n.) 情緒
4 disaster [dɪ'zæstɚ] (n.) 災難
5 feature ['fitʃɚ] (n.) 特徵
6 contrast ['kɑn͵træst] (n.) 對比
7 rush [rʌʃ] (v.) 衝
8 miserable ['mɪzərəbl] (a.) 悽慘的
9 grin [grɪn] (v.) 齜牙咧嘴

Chapter 4

Finally, one dark November night, I completed my work. I collected my instruments and gave life to the being[2] that lay at my feet. By the light of the candle, I saw the eyes of the creature open; it breathed hard, then made quick movements of its legs and arms.

How can I describe my emotions[3] when I saw this disaster[4] that with such endless work and care I had tried to create? I had selected his features[5] as beautiful. Beautiful?! Great God!! His yellow skin only just covered the muscles and veins beneath; he had shiny black hair; his teeth were pearly white. But these good features only made a more unpleasant contrast[6] with his watery eyes, his lined face and straight black lips.

I had worked hard for nearly two years but now that I had finished, the beauty of the dream had disappeared. Horror and disgust filled my heart.

I rushed[7] out of the room and lay on my bed and tried to forget about my creation. But when I awoke in the night, by the yellow light of the moon, I saw the miserable[8] monster I had created. He stood by my bed and looked at me. His mouth opened and he made a sound I could not understand, and grinned[9]. I rushed past him and spent the rest of the night walking up and down nervously outside.

14   At six o'clock I went out into the wet, gray streets, terrified[1] of meeting the creature at every corner. I hurried on, soaked[2] by the pouring rain. I came to an inn[3] where coaches[4] from other places stopped. To my surprise a Swiss coach stopped, and Henry Clerval got out.

"My dear Frankenstein!" he said. "I'm so glad you were here exactly when I arrived!"

I was delighted to see Clerval, my dear childhood friend. He brought back memories of my father, Elizabeth and all those scenes of home that were important to me. In a moment I forgot my horror and misery[5]. For the first time in many months, I felt calm and happy. We walked to my apartment, while Henry talked about our friends and families.

"But, my dear Frankenstein," he continued, "how thin and pale you are, as if you had been up for several nights."

"You are right," I replied. "Recently I have been so busy with one project that I have not allowed myself to rest, but it is finished now, and finally I am free."

I shook as we walked. I thought the creature might still be in my apartment, and I feared that Henry would see him. So I was delighted to find the apartment empty. We had breakfast, but I could not sit still. I jumped up, clapped my hands and laughed aloud.

"Victor!" Henry cried, "Don't laugh like that! How ill you are! What is the matter?"

---

1 terrify ['tɛrəˌfaɪ] (v.) 使害怕   4 coach [kotʃ] (n.) （舊時的）四輪大馬車
2 soak [sok] (v.) 浸泡；濕透   5 misery ['mɪzərɪ] (n.) 痛苦；不幸
3 inn [ɪn] (n.) 小旅館

"Don't ask me," I cried, putting my hands over my eyes. "Save me, save me!"

This was the start of a nervous fever which kept me in my room for several months. Henry was my only nurse. During my illness, the monster was always before my eyes, and I talked madly about him. Slowly I recovered and by the following spring, I felt much better.

"Dearest Clerval!" I said one morning. "How very good you are to me. Instead of studying, you have spent the whole winter in my sick room. How can I repay[1] you?"

"Get well as fast as you can," he replied. "And write a letter to your father and Elizabeth. They would be happy to receive a letter in your own handwriting."

"Of course I will," I said.

"Well since you feel so happy," he answered, "perhaps you would like to see this letter from Elizabeth? It has been here for some days."

The letter from Elizabeth said she was delighted to hear of my recovery[2], and hoped I would write soon. She told me that my father was very well and that my brother Ernest was now sixteen and wanted to become a soldier. My youngest brother William was now tall and attractive, with blue eyes and curly hair. She ended by saying how grateful they were that Henry had looked after me so well.

---

1 repay [rɪ`pe] (v.) 回報        3 abandon [ə`bændən] (v.) 拋棄
2 recovery [rɪ`kʌvərɪ] (n.) 恢復    4 Oriental [ˌorɪ`ɛntl] (a.) （大寫）東方的；亞洲的

Later, I introduced Henry to my university professors. I was embarrassed when both Mr Waldman and Mr Krempe talked highly of my work. But wanting to forget everything that had brought me to my nervous state and the creation of that monster, I abandoned[3] my previous studies. Instead I chose to follow Henry and his studies of Oriental[4] languages.

I had planned to return to Geneva in the autumn, but I didn't want to leave Clerval on his own in a strange place. And then the winter snows came and the roads were blocked. In May of the following year Henry and I went on a walking tour of the Ingolstadt region, spending two weeks exploring the area. It was a very happy time, with much good conversation, too, and I returned to Ingolstadt healthy and full of energy.

Chapter 5

(17)　When I returned home I found the following letter from my father:

My dear Victor,

You have probably been waiting for a letter from me to plan the date of your return. However, I'm afraid your return will not be a happy one. William is dead! Victor, he is murdered[1]!

Last Thursday Elizabeth, your two brothers and I went for a walk at Plainpalais. We went further than usual, but as we returned Elizabeth and I could not find Ernest and William. They were playing hide and seek[2]. Then Ernest returned saying he could not find William. We searched until night fell, then went home, thinking that perhaps he was there. He was not. We returned, with torches[3], to keep searching.

At about five in the morning, I discovered my lovely son, with the signs of the murderer's hands on his neck.

Elizabeth blamed herself[4], because she had let William wear a valuable necklace with a miniature[5] painting of his mother on it . . . and this was missing[6]. It was certainly what the murderer wanted.

Come home now and help us to get over[7] our deep feelings of sadness and loss[8].

Your affectionate father,
Alphonse Frankenstein

Tears poured from my eyes. I threw the letter down and indicated that Clerval should read it.

When he had finished, he said: "There is nothing I can say to help, my friend. This loss is a disaster you cannot repair. What are you going to do?"

"I'll go to Geneva straight away."

1 murder [ˈmɝdɚ] (v.) 謀殺
2 hide and seek（遊戲）捉迷藏
3 torch [tɔrtʃ] (n.) 火把
4 blame oneself 自責
5 miniature [ˈmɪnɪətʃɚ] (n.) 微型畫
6 missing [ˈmɪsɪŋ] (a.) 失蹤的
7 get over 恢復
8 loss [lɔs] (n.) 失落；損失

On my journey I was filled with mixed feelings: sadness at my little brother's death, and joy at seeing my father, Elizabeth and Ernest after nearly six years. When I finally saw Lake Geneva and the mountains around it I cried with happiness.

I decided to first visit Plainpalais where William had died. I went by boat across the lake and as I landed[1], a spectacular[2] thunderstorm started, growing stronger, with pouring rain and flashes of lightning illuminating[3] the lake. It raised my spirits[4], and I shouted: "William, dear Angel! This is your funeral[5] and your funeral song."

Suddenly, a flash of lightning illuminated a figure coming out from behind some trees. I could not be wrong. It was the horrible monster to which I had given life! How had he come here? Had he murdered my brother? I became sure that it was true. He continued past me, and in the next flash of lightning I saw him easily climbing the cliffs[6] of a nearby mountain.

I didn't move. The rain continued. It was now two years since he had received life. Had I created a creature that enjoyed killing and making others unhappy? I stayed there the whole night, wet and in a state of great worry. Was the creature going to destroy everything that was important to me?

---

1 land [lænd] (v.) 著陸
2 spectacular [spɛkˋtækjələ˞] (a.) 壯觀的
3 illuminate [ɪˋlumə͵net] (v.) 照亮

4 spirit [ˋspɪrɪt] (n.) 精神
5 funeral [ˋfjunərəl] (n.) 喪禮
6 cliff [klɪf] (n.) 懸崖

At five o'clock I arrived at my father's house, so I went into the library to rest. Some time later, my brother Ernest came in.

"Welcome, my dearest Victor," he said. "But I wish you had come three months ago and found us all happy. I hope you will comfort[1] our father, and stop Elizabeth blaming herself for William's death."

Tears poured from our eyes, as Ernest explained more about Elizabeth: "She accuses herself of having caused our brother's death, but since they have found the murderer . . ."

"Found the murderer!" I shouted. "Good God! How is that possible? Who could follow him? I saw him, too. He was free last night!"

"I do not know what you mean," replied my brother, much surprised, "because the discovery we have made completes our misery. Who would have thought that our servant[2] Justine Moritz, who was so kind and loving with all the family, could suddenly commit[3] such an awful crime[4]?"

Ernest explained that on the morning after William's murder, Justine had felt ill and was in bed for several days. One of the servants had examined the clothes she had worn on the night of the murder, and found the necklace with our mother's picture in a pocket. The servants went to the magistrate[5] and Justine was arrested and charged[6]. She was extremely confused, which made everyone think she was responsible.

(21)   "You are all wrong," I said. "I know the murderer. Justine is innocent[7]."

When my father entered a few moments later, Ernest exclaimed[8]: "Father—Victor says that he knows who murdered poor William."

"And so do we," said my father. "And I am sorry that one whom we loved and trusted should reward[9] us in this way."

"Justine is innocent," I said.

"If she is," my father replied, "we will find out today when she is tried[10] and set free[11]."

---

1   comfort [ˈkʌmfət] (v.) 使舒服；安慰

2   servant [ˈsɝvənt] (n.) 僕人

3   commit [kəˈmɪt] (v.) 犯（罪）

4   crime [kraɪm] (n.) 罪

5   magistrate [ˈmædʒɪsˌtret] (n.) 地方法官

6   charge [tʃɑrdʒ] (v.) 控告

7   innocent [ˈɪnəsn̩t] (a.) 無罪的

8   exclaim [ɪksˈklem] (v.) 大聲叫嚷

9   reward [rɪˈwɔrd] (v.) 報答

10   try [traɪ] (v.) 審判

11   set free 釋放

Chapter 6

Next morning we went to the law court[1]. Witnesses[2] reported several strange facts about Justine. She had been out the whole night of the murder. Then, towards morning, she was seen near where the body was found. She had been confused when asked what she was doing there. She had returned home about eight in the morning, saying she had looked for William. On seeing the body, she fell into violent[3] hysterics[4] and stayed in bed for several days. The necklace with the picture was found in her pocket by a servant.

Justine then defended[5] herself. She had passed the evening of the murder at an aunt's house, with Elizabeth's permission[6]. When she returned she heard William was missing and so went out to look for him. She was out for many hours. As Geneva city gates were shut she could not return home, so she slept in the barn of some people she knew, without disturbing them. The next morning she looked for William again. If she went near where the body was found, it was by chance. If she had appeared confused, it was because of her lack of sleep, and her worry about William. She could say nothing about the necklace.

(23) Then Elizabeth spoke: "I have lived in the same house as Justine for seven years. She looked after Madame Frankenstein in her final illness with great affection[7] and care. She was strongly attached[8] to William. As for the necklace— the main proof[9]—I would happily give it to her. I believe Justine is absolutely[10] innocent."

However, the crowd wanted someone to be responsible for this horrible murder, and the magistrate condemned[11] poor Justine. Next morning, they told me that she had confessed[12]. Later, we visited Justine in prison. She said she had only confessed so that she could receive absolution[13] and that she was ready to die.

I now felt that I was the true murderer.

---

1 court [kort] (n.) 法院
2 witness [ˋwɪtnɪs] (n.) 目擊者；證人
3 violent [ˋvaɪələnt] (a.) 猛烈的
4 hysterics [hɪsˋtɛrɪks] (n.) 歇斯底里
5 defend [dɪˋfɛnd] (v.) 辯護
6 permission [pɚˋmɪʃən] (n.) 許可；同意
7 affection [əˋfɛkʃən] (n.) 感情
8 attach [əˋtætʃ] (v.) 使喜愛

9 proof [pruf] (n.) 證據
10 absolutely [ˋæbsə͵lutlɪ] (adv.) 絕對地
11 condemn [kənˋdɛm] (v.) 譴責
12 confess [kənˋfɛs] (v.) 認罪
13 absolution [͵æbsəˋluʃən] (n.) (宗教的) 罪之赦免： (義務等的) 免除

After Justine's death, I looked around our once-happy family. Everyone was destroyed and in deepest misery because of the deaths of William and Justine, and it was all the work of my hands. I was unable to sleep. I had done terrible things. I had begun with good intentions[1]—to be useful to my fellow beings. But I had destroyed everything. Instead of looking back happily on my achievements[2] and looking forward with hope to[3] new discoveries, I felt only regret, horror, despair[4] and guilt.

REGRET

- Do you think Victor Frankenstein is right to feel this way? Why? Discuss in small groups.

1 intention [ɪnˈtɛnʃən] (n.) 意圖
2 achievement [əˈtʃivmənt] (n.) 成就
3 look forward to 期待
4 despair [dɪˈspɛr] (n.) 絕望
5 suffer [ˈsʌfɚ] (v.) 遭受；受苦
6 fear [fɪr] (v.) 害怕；擔心
7 thoughtlessly [ˈθɔtlɪslɪ] (adv.) 草率地；不加思索地
8 revenge [rɪˈvɛndʒ] (n.) 報仇；報復
9 exhausted [ɪgˈzɔstɪd] (a.) 精疲力竭的

Chapter 7

25   We then moved to our house beside the lake. At night I
often took the boat and passed many hours on the water. I
felt like throwing myself into the silent lake so that the water
would close over my miseries forever. But I stopped myself
by thinking of Elizabeth, whom I loved so sweetly, and who
suffered[5] so much.

Every day I feared[6] the monster would do some new evil
act. I had a feeling that he had not finished. I wished I could
kill the creature which I had so thoughtlessly[7] created. My
desire for revenge[8] and my hate of him filled my whole body
and mind. I wanted to take revenge for the deaths of William
and Justine.

Sometimes, in such states of passion, I needed physical
exercise and a change of place. So, in mid-August, I went
walking in the Alpine valleys near Chamonix. The weather was
fine, and the scenery of the Alps themselves was spectacular.
I felt pleasure amongst the wonders of nature, but then
my horror and despair would return. When I finally got to
Chamonix, both my mind and my body were exhausted[9], and
I slept deeply that night.

1 midday [ˋmɪdˌde] (n.) 正午；日中
2 glacier [ˋgleʃɚ] (n.) 冰河
3 peak [pik] (n.) 山頂；山峰
4 dare [dɛr] (v.) 敢；竟敢
5 duty [ˋdjutɪ] (n.) 職責
6 owe [o] (v.) 虧欠

The following morning, it was pouring with rain. The mountains were covered in thick cloud. But I set out to climb Montanvert. It was difficult on the narrow path, but by midday[1] I was at the top. The wind blew the cloud away, and I went down onto the glacier[2] and crossed it.

I could now see Mont Blanc. It was a spectacular view—the river of ice surrounded by icy peaks[3].

As I looked, I suddenly saw a large man coming towards me at superhuman speed. I realized that it was the monster I had created. I was filled with anger and horror, and decided to fight him to the death.

"Devil!" I shouted. "Do you dare[4] to come near me? Aren't you afraid that I will take my revenge?"

"I expected this," he said. "People hate all ugly things, and I am uglier than them all. But you, my creator, you want to kill me? How dare you play with life like this? Do your duty[5] towards me, and I will do my duty towards you and all mankind. If you agree, I will leave you and them in peace. If not, then I will kill and destroy all your remaining friends."

"Monster! Devil!" I screamed. "You blame me for your creation. Well, come here and let me end the life which I so thoughtlessly gave you!"

I jumped at him, but he easily moved out of the way, and said: "Please listen to me. I have suffered enough. I am your creature, and I will be gentle with you if you will give me what you owe[6] me. Oh, Frankenstein, don't be kind to everyone else and unkind to me alone. I see happiness everywhere which I cannot have. I was kind and good; misery made me into a monster. Make me happy and I'll be good."

"Go away!" I shouted. "I will not listen to you. We are enemies[1]. Go away, or let us fight until one of us dies."

"I really was good, but I am alone," he said. "If you hate me then what can I expect from others? The world hates me, so why should I not hate everyone? But you can change this. Come to the barn where I have made my shelter[2] and listen to my story before you judge me finally. It is in your power to save me. You can decide whether I lead a good life, or whether I become a devil for your fellow beings and the cause of your own destruction[3]. Listen to me, Frankenstein!"

Partly because I was curious and partly because I felt sorry for the monster, I followed him across the ice. Soon we were seated by the fire near his shelter and he began his tale.

LISTEN

- Do you think it is important to listen to a person's story before judging them? Why?

- Can you think of a time when you judged someone and then found out later that their story was completely different? How did you feel when you found out the real story? Tell a friend.

---

1 enemy [ˈɛnəmɪ] (n.) 敵人
2 shelter [ˈʃɛltɚ] (n.) 躲避處
3 destruction [dɪˈstrʌkʃən] (n.) 毀滅
4 cottage [ˈkɑtɪdʒ] (n.) 農舍；小屋
5 faint [fent] (v.) 昏厥；暈倒
6 attack [əˈtæk] (v.) 攻擊

Chapter 8

And so the monster began:

"At first I was confused by everything. I lived in the woods near Ingolstadt. Gradually, I learned to recognize the birds, insects, plants and trees. I once found a fire, left by others, and so I learnt how to keep myself warm at night. But I was very hungry, and I looked for food. I found a small barn where an old man was making breakfast. On seeing me, he screamed and ran away as fast as he could. I ate his breakfast, then I lay down and slept.

"I awoke at noon and walked on. At sunset I reached a village. It seemed wonderful—the barns, cottages[4] and bigger houses, many with milk and cheese in the windows. I entered one of the better houses, but the children screamed and one of the women fainted[5]. The whole village came: some ran away, and some attacked[6] me. I left.

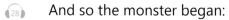

"Eventually, I found a small building next to an isolated[1] cottage. It was simple but dry. I was also able to look out through gaps[2] in the walls, and see into the cottage through a gap in one of them. A little later, a young woman arrived. A young man met her and they went into the cottage. Inside the room I saw an old man who looked very unhappy. The girl was doing various jobs. Then she gave the old man a guitar and he began to play, while she sang. It was beautiful. The young man returned later with wood for the fire, a loaf and cheese. The girl cooked some plants from the garden, and they all ate. Then night fell and the family went to sleep.

"I thought about what I had seen and the people's gentle manners[3]. I wanted to join them, but I decided to stay there quietly, to observe[4] and understand them. I watched them working. I also noticed that the young man and woman treated the old man with love and respect, but sometimes they went off together and cried. I couldn't understand why.

"Later I understood that they were very poor and hungry. Previously[5] I had sometimes stolen their food, but after that I lived on what I could find from the woods. I also helped them. I cut wood for them at night, as the young man spent much of the day looking for wood for the fire. At first they were very surprised, but then they spent the days repairing the cottage and working in the garden.

---

1 isolated [ˈaɪslˌetɪd] (a.) 孤立的
2 gap [gæp] (n.) 裂縫
3 manners [ˈmænɚz] (n.) 態度
4 observe [əbˈzɝv] (v.) 觀察
5 previously [ˈpriviəslɪ] (adv.) 以前

"Through watching and listening to them I learnt a lot of basic words, and also the names of the three: *father*; *brother* or *son* or *Felix*; *sister* or *Agatha*.

"As the winter progressed[1], I learnt more of their words. The father was blind, so the son sometimes read to him. I wanted to meet these sweet, kind people, but I realized that I needed to be able to use their language well. I admired their beauty and I knew that I was monstrous[2] because I had seen myself reflected[3] in a pool of water.

"My daily life was almost always the same. I watched the people in the morning, slept in the middle of the day, watched them again in the afternoon and evening, and then if it was a clear night, I went out into the woods to collect my own food, and to cut wood for them. As spring arrived I had happy feelings in my heart.

"One day, a lady arrived at the cottage. When Felix saw her, his sadness disappeared and a great change began in their lives. She met his sister and father, but she could not speak their language, nor they hers. They started teaching her their language and so I followed them very carefully. The lady was called Safie, and she and I improved[4] our language quickly. I also learned to read as she did, and learnt about history and society through the book that Felix used to teach her.

"However, I also realized that I was lower than the lowest human. There was no one like me. Was I a monster that all men ran from and nobody wanted? The gentle words of Agatha and Safie were not for me, nor the conversation of the old man and Felix. They talked of families, friends and children, but where were mine? My past life was completely empty. I had always been the same height and size, and I had never seen another being like me. What was I?"

PAST

- Can you imagine not having a past? How would you feel? Tell a friend about your past.

1 progress [prə`grɛs] (v.) 前進；進行
2 monstrous [`mɑnstrəs] (a.) 似怪物的
3 reflect [rɪ`flɛkt] (v.) 映現
4 improve [ɪm`pruv] (v.) 增進；改善

Chapter 9

The monster continued:

"After a time, I realized that although there were similarities[1] between me and human beings, there was one big difference: I was dependent on nobody and had no relatives[2]. Nobody would miss me when I was gone. I was ugly to look at and very big. What did this mean? Who was I? What was I? Where did I come from?

"But as I could now read, I looked at some papers of yours which I had kept. They were the four months of your journal before my creation. You described everything in detail. It showed your horror at what you were doing. I felt sicker and sicker as I read it. I wondered why you had created a monster so horrible that even you turned away in disgust. But my neighbors were so good that I wanted to be their friend, to take part in[3] their happiness. I had seen that they never turned away poor people who stopped at their door, and felt they would not turn me away in horror.

"I thought of how I could introduce myself to them. I decided it would be best to enter the cottage when the blind old man was alone. I knew that my hideous[4] appearance was the main cause of people's horror. I felt that if I could get the old man on my side, the younger neighbors might tolerate[5] me. Then one sunny winter's afternoon Safie, Agatha and Felix went for a long country walk, and I took my chance. I knocked at the cottage door.

'Who is there?' asked the old man. 'Come in.'

I entered. 'Excuse me,' I said, 'I am a traveler in need of rest. Could I sit by your fire for a few minutes?'

'Come in,' said the old man, 'I am blind and my children are away from home, so I cannot find food for you. Are you French?'

1　similarity [ˌsɪməˈlærətɪ] (n.) 相似點
2　relative [ˈrɛlətɪv] (n.) 親戚
3　take part in 參加……
4　hideous [ˈhɪdɪəs] (a.) 駭人的
5　tolerate [ˈtɑləˌret] (v.) 包容

'No,' I replied, 'but I was educated by a French family. I now want to get protection from some friends whom I love, and whom I hope will help me. But they have never seen me, and I am afraid, because if I cannot make friends with them, I will be alone in the world forever.'

'That is very sad,' he answered. 'If you tell me your story perhaps I can help.'

'Thank you,' I said happily. 'I accept your generous offer[1]. I hope that with your help they will not send me away.'

'May I know the names of these friends and where they live?' he asked.

I took his hand and said: 'You and your family are these friends. Do not leave me to suffer alone.'

'Great God!' exclaimed the old man. 'Who are you?'

"At that moment, the cottage door opened and Felix, Safie and Agatha entered. It is impossible to describe their horror on seeing me. Agatha fainted, Safie rushed out of the cottage, and Felix jumped forward, and pulled his father from me, pushing me to the ground and hitting me violently with a stick. My heart sank and I felt sick. I was filled with pain and worry. I left the cottage, and managed to get back into my home without being seen.

"Oh my damned[2] creator! I was in such misery. When night came, I went out into the woods, wandering[3] and howling[4]. There was nobody who would feel pity for me or help me. I declared[5] war against human beings, and more than all against my creator who had sent me out to face this terrible misery. After dark I went back to my home.

"Later, Felix appeared with another man, and I listened to their conversation.

'Do you realize that you will have to pay three months' rent[6] and lose the produce of your garden?' asked the man.

'We can never live in your cottage again after the events I described to you,' said Felix. 'Please, take back your cottage, and let me leave this place as quickly as possible.'

"I never saw the family again. My only link[7] to the world had gone. Feelings of revenge and hatred filled me. First, I destroyed everything in the garden. And then I set fire to the cottage.

MONSTER

- Do you feel anger or pity for the monster?

1 offer ['ɔfɚ] (n.) 提供
2 damned [dæmd] (a.) 被詛咒的；討厭的
3 wander ['wɑndɚ] (v.) 漫遊；閒逛
4 howl [haʊl] (v.) 嗥叫；怒吼
5 declare [dɪ'klɛr] (v.) 宣布
6 rent [rɛnt] (n.) 租金
7 link [lɪŋk] (n.) 聯繫

"I decided to look for you next. You were the only one who I could ask for pity. I knew from your journal that you lived in Geneva. But how could I find the way? The sun was my only guide as I could not ask directions from any humans. My travels were long and I suffered greatly. It was late autumn when I started out, traveling only at night to avoid[1] meeting anyone. It rained and snowed, great rivers became frozen, and the earth was cold and bare[2]. By early spring I reached Switzerland.

"One day, I was traveling through a forest. I did not hide and rest as usual, because it was so beautiful and I felt happy. I came to a deep, fast river when I heard voices, so I ran behind a tree.

"A little girl ran along laughing, but slipped[3] and fell into the river. I climbed down with great difficulty to save her. She was unconscious[4], and I was trying to help her when the man who had been with her appeared. He rushed up and grabbed[5] the girl from me and ran off. I followed him, without knowing why, but he turned round and shot me.

"That was my reward! I had saved a human life, and now I was in pain. I decided to hate all humans, and to get revenge whenever I could. After several weeks in the wood, the wound[6] in my shoulder healed[7].

---

1 avoid [əˈvɔɪd] (v.) 避開
2 bare [bɛr] (a.) 光禿禿的
3 slip [slɪp] (v.) 滑倒
4 unconscious [ʌnˈkɑnʃəs] (a.) 不省人事的

5 grab [græb] (v.) 抓住
6 wound [wund] (n.) 傷口
7 heal [hil] (v.) 痊癒

"Then I traveled on towards Geneva, and hid in the fields nearby to decide what I should do to you.

"While I was there I was disturbed by the arrival of a beautiful child. I suddenly thought that he was innocent and would not be afraid of me. If I took him, I could educate him as my friend, and I would not be so lonely in the world. So I caught the boy as he passed. As soon as he saw me, he screamed and covered his eyes. I removed[1] his hand from his face.

'I do not want to hurt you,' I said. 'Listen to me.'

'Let me go!' he cried. 'You're an ugly monster. You want to eat me. Let me go or I'll tell my father.'

---

1 remove [rɪˋmuv] (v.) 移去
2 victim [ˋvɪktɪm] (n.) 受害者

54

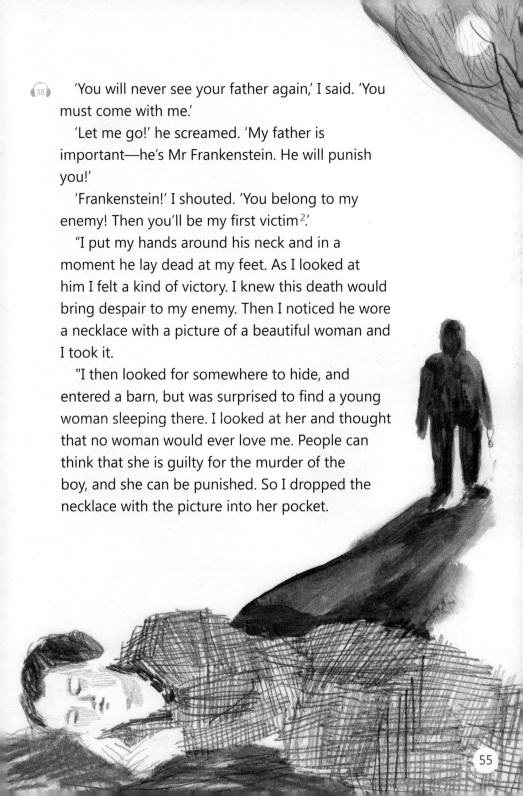

'You will never see your father again,' I said. 'You must come with me.'

'Let me go!' he screamed. 'My father is important—he's Mr Frankenstein. He will punish you!'

'Frankenstein!' I shouted. 'You belong to my enemy! Then you'll be my first victim².'

"I put my hands around his neck and in a moment he lay dead at my feet. As I looked at him I felt a kind of victory. I knew this death would bring despair to my enemy. Then I noticed he wore a necklace with a picture of a beautiful woman and I took it.

"I then looked for somewhere to hide, and entered a barn, but was surprised to find a young woman sleeping there. I looked at her and thought that no woman would ever love me. People can think that she is guilty for the murder of the boy, and she can be punished. So I dropped the necklace with the picture into her pocket.

39 "I stayed around that area, but eventually I wandered towards these mountains, where I have remained ever since. I am alone and miserable. Humans will have nothing to do with me, but a female as deformed[1] and horrible as myself would not refuse me. My companion[2] must be of the same species as myself. You must create this being."

He finished talking and stared at me. I only felt my anger at William's death.

"I refuse," I said. "Why should I create another creature for you both to do terrible things in the world? Go away!"

"You are wrong," he replied. "I am evil because I am miserable. Everyone hates me, so why should I pity them when they do not pity me? And if I cannot make people love me, then I will make them fear me. And my revenge will mainly be aimed[3] at you. Be careful, or I will destroy you."

LOVE

- Do you think love stops people from being bad? Discuss in small groups.

I thought about what he had said, and realized that maybe if he was happy, he would not create problems for others again.

"If I agree," I said, "swear[4] that you will leave Europe forever as soon as I give you a female to go with you."

"I swear," he cried. "If you agree you will never see me again. Now go and start your work. I'll watch your progress carefully, and when you are ready I will appear."

He left and descended[5] the mountain very quickly. I returned immediately to Geneva. I felt very unhappy about the whole situation[6] before me, and could find almost no happiness when I saw my family again. To save them, I had to perform this awful task[7].

TASK

- What does Victor Frankenstein have to do?
- Why is it so awful?

---

1 deformed [dɪˈfɔrmd] (a.) 畸形的
2 companion [kəmˈpænjən] (n.) 伴侶
3 aim [em] (v.) 瞄準
4 swear [swɛr] (v.) 發誓
   （三態：swear; swore; sworn）
5 descend [dɪˈsɛnd] (v.) 往下走；下降
6 situation [ˌsɪtʃuˈeʃən] (n.) 情況；處境
7 task [tæsk] (n.) 任務；苦差事

Chapter 10

Many weeks passed, but I was unable to start my work. I was frightened that the monster would come, and I felt disgusted by what I had promised to do. One day my father said he wanted to talk to me.

"Victor, I have always looked forward to your marriage to Elizabeth. You have always been close to each other, so I wonder whether you now see her more as a sister and a friend?"

"Don't worry, father," I replied. "I hope that one day Elizabeth and I will get married."

"This is wonderful news," he replied. "Are you interested in getting married soon?"

I thought of my promise to the creature. How could I get married and have a normal life before I had fulfilled[1] my terrible promise? I would need to hide somewhere secret to complete the horrible task. These feelings helped me answer my father's question. I said I needed to go to England first, without saying exactly why, for a period of up to a year. My father was happy to agree, hoping that the change would complete my physical and mental[2] recovery.

---

1   fulfill [fʊlˋfɪl] (v.) 履行   3   absence [ˋæbsns] (n.) 缺席
2   mental [ˋmɛntl] (a.) 心理的   4   remote [rɪˋmot] (a.) 遙遠的

In September, I left for England. I was worried the monster might hurt my family in my absence[3], but believed that he would follow me to England, and so they would be safe. Henry Clerval came with me. We sailed down the Rhine to Rotterdam and got a ship to London.

In London I met an important natural philosopher to find new information related to my unpleasant task. Henry was interested in going to India and started collecting information on how to organize it, while I gathered the materials I needed. We slowly made our way to Perth in Scotland, where we had been invited by a friend.

I was worried because I had still not started my work. I wondered what the creature might do. I left Clerval with our friend in Perth while I went to complete my task in a cottage on a remote[4] island in the Orkneys further north. As time passed, I found it increasingly difficult to continue with my horrible work, and every moment I expected to look up and see the form of the monster before me.

Chapter 11

One night, I was thinking about what I was doing. I had no idea what this female creature might be like. My first creation had promised to leave Europe, but she might not agree. She might be even more evil than he was. And if they had children, then what race[1] of creatures would I have started on earth?

I suddenly looked up and saw the monster outside, looking at me and grinning. He had followed me and was waiting for my work to end. But in his face I saw only evil. I thought how mad my promise to him had been. Trembling[2] with fear, I tore[3] the thing I had created to pieces before him. With a horrible howl of despair, he disappeared.

I went back to my own room. I heard footsteps and the sound of the door and I knew the monster had come.

"You destroyed your work," he said. "Do you dare to break your promise? I have been waiting and now you have destroyed my hopes."

---

1 race [res] (n.) 種族
2 tremble ['trɛmbl] (v.) 顫抖
3 tear [tɛr] (v.) 撕碎（三態：tear; tore; torn）

"Go away!" I shouted. "I have broken my promise. I will never make another evil creature like you."

"Remember that I have power," he said. "I can make your situation even worse. You are my creator, but I am your master. Obey!"

"You cannot make me do something wicked[1]. I will not create an an evil companion for you." I shouted. "Go away!"

"You will regret this," cried the creature. "Now, I am only interested in revenge. Remember this: I will be with you on your wedding night."

"Monster!" I screamed. "Before you think of killing me, make sure that you are safe yourself."

He left quickly, and I later saw him sailing away in his boat. Then I started thinking of his threat: *I will be with you on your wedding night.* So I had until then to do something.

Two days later a letter from Clerval arrived, asking me to come back so we could return to London to complete his Indian business. I went to my laboratory and packed up all my instruments. I put all the horrible mess[2] of my work into a basket and filled it with stones. Later that night I sailed out to sea and dropped it over the side of my boat.

It was a peaceful, moonlit night, and I fell asleep on the boat. When I awoke the wind and waves were very strong. I could not control the boat, so I let the wind carry it. I looked at the clouds moving fast in the sky and then at the sea and I thought that I was going to die. Much, much later I was pleased to see land. It was calmer now, and I followed the coast until I came to a small harbor. People soon gathered around as I tied up the boat.

"Excuse me," I started, hearing them speak English. "Can you tell me where I am, please?"

"You will know that soon enough," said one man.

"Why do you answer me so rudely[3]?" I asked.

"Because it is the custom[4] of the Irish to hate bad people," he replied. "You must follow me to Mr Kirwin to explain yourself."

"Who is Mr Kirwin?" I asked. "And why must I explain myself?"

"Mr Kirwin is the magistrate," he said. "And you are to explain the death of a man who was found murdered here last night."

I was very surprised by this answer, and although exhausted and very hungry, I followed him, ready to prove[5] my innocence.

IRELAND

- Victor Frankenstein is now in Ireland. Look at a map or on the Internet to follow his journey on the sea from the Orkney Islands to the northern coast of Ireland.

1 wicked ['wɪkɪd] (a.) 壞的；缺德的
2 mess [mɛs] (n.) 凌亂
3 rudely ['rudlɪ] (adv.) 無禮地
4 custom ['kʌstəm] (n.) 習俗
5 prove [pruv] (v.) 證明

Chapter 12

I was taken before the magistrate, who called for witnesses. A sailor explained how the night before they had returned to land some distance from the town, because of the strong winds and storm. They had found the still-warm body of a young man. Someone had strangled[1] him. On hearing this I shook, remembering my brother William.

Other witnesses saw a boat like mine with a single man in it near the place. I was then taken in to see the body. Imagine my feelings when I saw that it was Henry Clerval!

"Has my murderous[2] behavior killed you, too, Henry?" I shouted. "I have already destroyed two. But you, Clerval, my friend, my helper . . ."

I fainted and was carried from the room. I lay in a bed for two months at the point of death, raving[3] about murdering William, Justine and now Clerval.

Then one day I woke to find myself in prison. Kirwin visited me occasionally[4], to see how I was. One day he told me that my father was there.

---

1 strangle ['stræŋgl̩] (v.) 勒死
2 murderous ['mɜ˞dərəs] (a.) 殘忍的
3 rave [rev] (v.) 狂罵；胡言亂語
4 occasionally [ə'keʒənl̩ɪ] (adv.) 偶爾

5 mood [mud] (n.) 心情
6 misery ['mɪzərɪ] (n.) 痛苦；不幸
7 reject [rɪ'dʒɛkt] (v.) 駁回

My father gave me news that Elizabeth, Ernest and he were safe and well. After this first visit, my illness gradually left me, but my black mood[5] got worse. I had horrible images of the murdered Henry before me all the time. I hoped that I would be punished for the crime, and so end my own misery[6].

I was in prison for three months before the court heard my case. The jury rejected[7] it because there was proof that I was still on Orkney at the time when my friend's body was found, and soon I was set free from prison.

I wanted to return to Geneva quickly, so that I could look after the three people I loved so much. I wanted a chance to find where the monster was hiding, or if he dared to come to see me again, then to kill him.

Of course I frequently remembered the creature's words: *I will be with you on your wedding night.* This is what would happen: he would kill me on that night. His power over me would end. I would finally be a free man.

But this did not mean he would do nothing else before then. He had proved this by murdering Clerval.

Back in Geneva I was mostly in very low spirits and only Elizabeth was able to cheer me up[1]. We decided to get married in ten days' time. Arrangements for the wedding were made, and I prepared myself for the creature's attack. I carried pistols[2] and a knife with me constantly[3].

But as the days passed and the ceremony[4] was closer, I began to hope that all might be well.

After the ceremony, there was a large party at my father's house. We, however, went to Evian by boat, where we had planned to spend the night.

---

1 cheer someone up 使某人振作精神
2 pistol [ˋpɪstl̩] (n.) 手槍
3 constantly [ˋkɑnstəntlɪ] (adv.) 不斷地
4 ceremony [ˋsɛrəˏmonɪ] (n.) 典禮
5 corridor [ˋkɔrɪdɚ] (n.) 走廊
6 dreadful [ˋdrɛdfəl] (a.) 可怕的

Chapter 13

We landed at eight o'clock, walked for a short time on the shore, enjoying the evening light, then returned to the inn where we were staying. A heavy rainstorm started and my fears returned. I held the pistol I was carrying and decided I would fight until either I or the creature were dead.

I then thought how awful it would be for Elizabeth to see me fight to the death, so I asked her to go to bed. I continued walking along the corridors[5], looking for my enemy.

Suddenly I heard a dreadful[6] scream. I rushed to our room and entered. Elizabeth was dead! The murderer had thrown her on the bed. I fainted and woke some time later.

I then got up and held Elizabeth's cold body, and saw the mark of the monster's hands on her neck. Then as I looked out of the window, I saw him there, grinning and pointing at my dead wife.

I rushed to the window and fired my pistol. He ran quickly to the lake and jumped in. People came running when they heard the gun shot. We followed but found nothing.

I returned immediately to Geneva fearing that my father and Ernest were in danger. When I arrived, they were still alive. My father, however, was shocked by the news about Elizabeth, and a few days later he died of sadness.

I told my story to a magistrate in Geneva, saying I knew who had destroyed my family, and asking him to find and capture[1] the murderer. He listened in disbelief[2] and horror. Finally he said he would happily look for the creature, but that as he seemed to have superhuman strength, he was not sure how capture would be possible. He said I should be prepared to be disappointed.

I told him that I wanted revenge, and if he could not help me, then I would do it myself.

I now hated Geneva. I left, taking money and jewels[3] which had belonged to my mother. I started these wanderings which will only stop when I die. I have travelled everywhere and I will not rest until my enemy is dead.

---

1 capture [ˈkæptʃɚ] (v.) 捕獲；俘虜
2 disbelief [ˌdɪsbəˈlif] (n.) 不相信；懷疑
3 jewel [ˈdʒuəl] (n.) 寶石飾物

Before leaving I went to the cemetery where William, Elizabeth and my father were buried. I stood by their graves[1] and said out loud: "I promise that I will live until I have taken revenge on this horrible monster, and made him feel the misery that I now feel."

I heard a loud, evil laugh and then I heard the hated voice say:

"I am pleased, miserable man, that you have decided to live."

In the moonlight I saw him running away faster than any human could.

I followed him down the Rhône, over the Mediterranean[2] and across Russia. I was often cold, hungry and exhausted. Sometimes the monster left signs[3] for me—an arrow to show the direction he had taken, or a message: "You live. My power is complete. Follow me. I am going to the frozen north, where you will feel the misery of cold and frost[4], which I do not feel. You will have many hard, miserable hours before we fight for our lives."

I bought a sledge and dogs, and was able to catch up with[5] him. When I got to the sea, I was only one day behind him.

He had arrived the night before and had taken the villagers' sledge, dogs and all their winter food. He had set off across the frozen sea in a direction which did not lead to land. They believed he would die soon, either by the cold or because of the breaking ice.

---

1 grave [grev] (n.) 墓穴
2 Mediterranean [ˌmɛdətəˈreniən] (n.) 地中海
3 sign [saɪn] (n.) 符號；記號
4 frost [frɒst] (n.) 嚴寒
5 catch up with 趕上

I exchanged my sledge for one that would go better on the frozen sea, and bought a lot of food. Then I left the land. Sometimes mountains of ice blocked[1] my way, and at other times I heard the ice melting[2], only for it to freeze again. Often I feared that I would never catch my enemy before I died, but then after struggling[3] up some hill of ice I would see him in the distance, and I felt hopeful again. I got closer, and after two more days I was less than two kilometers behind him.

FOLLOW

- Follow Frankenstein and the monster's journey on a map.

But just when I thought I would catch him, the ice started breaking up. Soon there was open sea between me and my enemy. I was in despair until I saw your ship. I directed my ice "island" towards you. I was going to ask you for a boat in which to follow the monster. But you were going north, and you saved me from death. I was very pleased about this because my work was not yet completed.

---

1 block [blɑk] (v.) 阻礙
2 melt [mɛlt] (v.) 融化
3 struggle [ˋstrʌgl] (v.) 掙扎

But if I die without having caught him, and you find him, Walton, promise me that you will kill him for me, to take revenge for the deaths of William, Justine, Clerval, Elizabeth and my father. And mine.

WALTON

- Who is Walton? Go back to page 13 to check.

Conclusion

Robert Walton finished writing Victor Frankenstein's story at the end of August 17—. He then went on to tell his sister what happened over the following few weeks.

August 26th, 17—

My dear sister,

You have read this strange and terrifying story. Do you feel your blood run cold[1] with horror as mine does?

Currently I am surrounded by ice which might break the ship at any moment. It is extremely cold, and several of my men have already died. Some sailors asked me to promise that when the ship was free, we go south.

But Frankenstein asked them why they had come so far only to turn back; he praised[2] their courage, and said they would be heroes when they found the way through the ice to the Pacific Ocean, which was the aim of the expedition. He begged them to continue.

54

I asked them to consider what Frankenstein had said, but told them I would not continue further north if they decided against it.

September 9th, 17—

The ice began to move. By this time Frankenstein was very weak.

September 11th, 17—

We were completely free of the ice, and a passage to the south opened up. When the sailors saw this, they shouted with pleasure. This awoke Frankenstein, who asked why they were shouting.

"Because they will soon return to England," I replied.

"Are you really returning?" he asked.

"I'm afraid so," I answered. "I cannot lead them into danger when they do not want to go."

1 blood run cold 感到懼怕和恐怖
2 praise [prez] (v.) 稱讚

"Do what you want, Walton," he said, "but I will not go. My purpose is clear and I must follow my enemy."

I called the ship's doctor. He said that Frankenstein had only a few hours left to live. Some time later he called me to him and said: "Walton, I still wish for the death of my enemy. I created him, and I should kill him, but I have failed. Please promise me that you will kill him if you find him. The fact that he is still alive to do evil things when I am close to death, worries me."

He died a few minutes later. I went out to get some fresh air. It was midnight and the ship was sailing towards England. Suddenly, I heard horrible sounds coming from my cabin. I ran downstairs and opened the door. There was the creature that Frankenstein had described, gigantic[1] and ugly.

He jumped towards the window when I entered. I have never seen anything more unpleasant than his face.

The monster looked at me and pointed towards Frankenstein.

"He is my victim, too," he said. "With his death it is all finished. Oh, Frankenstein, can I ask you to forgive me now, after I destroyed you by destroying all you loved? But he is cold. He cannot answer me."

"You have carried your revenge too far," I said, "Frankenstein is now dead, thanks to you."

---

1 gigantic [dʒaɪˈɡæntɪk] (a.) 巨大的

"Do you think I enjoyed it?" asked the monster.
"When I returned to Switzerland, I pitied Frankenstein.
I hated myself. But when I discovered that he dared
to hope for happiness in things which I could never
enjoy, I felt jealous. Then I wanted revenge for all my
misery. This became my only passion. And now it is
ended. There is my last victim!"

"Monster!" I cried. "You do not feel pity. You are
shouting only because the victim is dead and no longer
in your power."

"That is not true," he interrupted. "I once had
dreams of being accepted by people for what I was
like, not for my appearance. Crime has made me lower
than the lowest, but even the worst criminals have
family and friends. And here I am without a friend in
the world. Alone.

"You seem to know my story. Why am I hated, and
not Felix who drove me away, or the father who shot
me when I saved his child? They are all good people,
and only I am not. This is all so unfair and makes me
very angry.

"It is true that I am terrible. I killed the young and
innocent, those who never hurt me, and I made my
creator's life a misery. There he lies, white and cold in
death.

57

"You hate me, but your hate is not more than the hate I feel for myself. Do not worry, I will do no more wrong. My work is nearly complete. I will leave your ship on a piece of ice and find some wood to make a funeral fire. I will burn myself on the fire so that nobody else can find and recreate a creature like me. Only in death can I find rest and peace. Goodbye!"

And with this he jumped out of the cabin window onto the piece of ice which lay below and was soon carried away into the darkness.

ⓐ Personal Response

1 Did you enjoy reading the story? Why?/Why not?

2 What did you think of the ending of the story?

3 Did you feel sorry for the monster? Why?/Why not? Give your reasons and discuss with a partner.

4 Did you feel sorry for Victor Frankenstein? Did he deserve all the terrible things that happened to him?

5 Have you seen a film version of *Frankenstein*? Was the story different from the film or TV versions of *Frankenstein* you have seen? Make a list of the differences. Discuss with a partner. Which version did you prefer?

6 Does the story have a message for us? If so, what is it? Discuss in a pairs; then share with another pair.

7 The monster says: "Please listen to me. I have suffered enough. I am your creature, and I will be gentle with you if you give me what you owe me . . . Make me happy and I'll be good." Do you think the monster was capable of keeping this promise to be good?

8 What do you think of the way Frankenstein behaved towards the monster? Could he have done anything differently? Write a few sentences and discuss with a partner.

❸ Comprehension

9 Tick (✓) true (T) or false (F).

T F (a) At the University of Ingolstadt, Frankenstein studied geography.

T F (b) After Frankenstein created the monster he was filled with horror and disgust.

T F (c) Elizabeth was Frankenstein's nurse when he was ill.

T F (d) Frankenstein's father wrote to say his brother Ernest was dead.

T F (e) Frankenstein went to the monster's shelter to hear his story.

T F (f) The monster asked Frankenstein to make him a female companion.

T F (g) Frankenstein did not agree to do this.

T F (h) Frankenstein destroyed the female after he saw the monster looking at him.

T F (i) The monster killed Henry Clerval when he and Frankenstein were in France.

T F (j) Elizabeth was murdered by the monster just before the wedding.

T F (k) Frankenstein left Geneva and followed the monster across Russia.

T F (l) Frankenstein was in the North Pole when he was picked up by Walton.

T F (m) After Frankenstein died the monster came onto the ship.

T F (n) The monster was happy that Frankenstein was dead.

10 Frankenstein tells his story to Walton. Complete the sentences with the following words.

> hate revenge letter science night monster deaths

a I threw myself into the study of mathematics and _____.

b I wanted to produce a new species. I worked day and _____.

c But when I saw the _____, horror and disgust filled my heart.

d Two years later I received a _____ saying that my brother William was murdered.

e I looked around our once-happy family. Everyone was destroyed because of the _____ of William and Justine.

f My desire for revenge and my _____ of him filled my body and mind.

g I beg you that you will kill him for me, to take _____.

11 Ask and answer these questions with a friend.

a Why did Frankenstein spend days and nights in tombs?
b Why was the monster so tall?
c What promise did Frankenstein make to the monster and then break?

12 What are these things and how were they important in the story? Make notes; then compare answers with a partner.

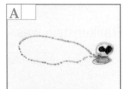

C Characters

13 Complete the sentences with the correct characters.

> William   Justine Moritz   old blind man   Elizabeth
> monster   Walton   Mr Krempe and Mr Waldman

a Frankenstein tells his story to _____ as a warning.

b Frankenstein's childhood was happy, especially after _____ became part of his family.

c _____ were Frankenstein's professors at university.

d Ernest and _____ were the names of Frankenstein's brothers.

e Frankenstein sometimes gave his creature names like "_____" and "devil."

f _____ was the nanny who was executed for William's murder.

g The _____ lived in the cottage with Felix, Agatha and Safie.

14 Frankenstein says his idea was to: "break through the knowledge of life and death and bring light into our dark world. I wanted to produce a new species that would bless me as its creator." What does he mean? Tick (✓).

_____ a He wants to make a new race of people who will thank him.

_____ b He wants to make a new species for the good of all humans.

15 The monster says: "Misery made me into a monster. Make me happy and I'll be good." What does he mean? Tick (✓).

_____ a I behave badly because I am sad. If you are kind to me, I'll be a nice person.

_____ b You created an evil monster, but you should have made a good one.

16 Do you think the monster behaves badly because Victor is not kind to him? Why?/Why not? Discuss with a partner.

17 What do we learn about the monster in these parts of the story? Make notes.

a When he watches the people in the cottage.

b When he saves the little girl who falls in the river and a man shoots him.

c When Frankenstein destroys the female monster he is making.

d When Frankenstein dies on Walton's ship.

18 Read and say who is talking, Frankenstein or the monster.

A

But when I saw him, horror and disgust filled my heart.

☐ Frankenstein ☐ monster

B

When night came, I went out into the woods, wandering and howling. There was nobody who would feel pity for me or help me.

☐ Frankenstein ☐ monster

C

Every day I feared he would do some new evil act.

☐ Frankenstein ☐ monster

D

Do you dare to break your promise?

☐ Frankenstein ☐ monster

❶ Plot and Theme

19 Put the events from the story in the correct order.

_____ a But when he saw the monster, he was horrified and disgusted.

_____ b Justine Moritz was executed for William's murder.

_____ c Frankenstein grew up in Geneva and had a happy childhood.

_____ d He studied natural philosophy and chemistry at university.

_____ e The monster killed Elizabeth on her wedding night.

_____ f His brother William was murdered by the monster.

_____ g He discovered the cause of life and decided to make his own creation.

_____ h His friend Henry Clerval was found dead, murdered by the monster.

_____ i He followed the monster across Europe and Russia to the North Pole.

_____ j The monster vowed to kill himself and disappeared into the darkness.

_____ k Frankenstein died and Walton found the monster on his ship.

_____ l He went back to Geneva and made plans to marry Elizabeth.

20 In pairs, answer the questions.

a. Why did Frankenstein tell Walton his story?

b. What misfortune occurred in Frankenstein's life when he was seventeen?

c. How did Frankenstein react when he saw his creation?

d. Why did the monster enter the cottage when the blind man was alone?

e. How did the monster die?

21 Read the quotation and discuss the questions with a partner.

> "There was no-one like me. They talked of families, friends and children, but where were mine? My past life was completely empty. I had always been the same height and size, and I had never seen another being like me. What was I?"

a. How was the monster different from humans?

b. What things did the monster want?
Find examples in the story.

22 Being ugly or different and how we treat people who are different is one of the themes of the story. Have you been in a situation where you felt different from other people around you? (Think of age, gender, race, etc.) How did you feel?

E Language

23 Complete this table with the words in the box.

Word box
graves
mathematics
regret
philosophy
funeral
deathbed
horror
joy
professor
chemistry
experiments
cemetery
despair
lectures
decay
disgust
anguish
murderer
science
tombs

University

Emotions

Death

24 Complete the sentences with words from Exercise **23**.

a) However, I decided not to go to his _____
because Mr Krempe was an ugly, short, fat man.

b) Mr Waldman's first lecture began with a history of
_____ and recent developments.

c) I spent days and nights in _____ watching
the _____ of human bodies.

d) I collected bones from the _____, and the
dissecting room and the slaughterhouse provided other
parts I needed.

e) On my journey I was filled with mixed feelings: sadness
at my little brother's death, and _____ at
seeing my father.

25 Complete the sentences with the correct form of the past
perfect.

a) I _____ (work) hard for nearly two years,
but now the beauty of the dream _____
(disappear).

b) I _____ (begin) with good intentions.
But I _____ (destroy) everything.

c) When I awoke in the night, I saw the miserable monster
I _____ (create).

d) Next morning they told me, Justine _____
(confess).

e) I told him about the very large man we
_____ (see) the day before.

26 Match the words to their definitions.

_____ [a] agony   [1] bad luck

_____ [b] misery   [2] reason for doing something

_____ [c] purpose   [3] good behavior

_____ [d] morals   [4] not nice

_____ [e] misfortune   [5] pain

_____ [f] unpleasant   [6] great sadness

27 Change these sentences from direct to indirect speech.

[a] "You are all wrong," I said. "I know the murderer. Justine is innocent."

_____

_____

[b] "Go away!" I shouted. "I will not listen to you! We are enemies."

_____

_____

[c] "I promise that I will live until I have taken revenge on this horrible monster."

_____

_____

[d] "I swear," he cried. "If you agree you will never see me again. Now go and start your work.

_____

_____

TEST

1 Listen and tick (✓) the correct picture.

a

1

2

b

1

2

c

1

2

d

1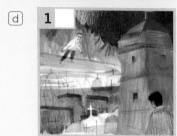

2

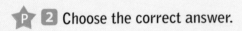 **2** Choose the correct answer.

_____ a Where was Walton sailing to when he saw Frankenstein?
1 Geneva.
2 Russia.
3 The North Pole.
4 The Orkneys.

_____ b When the monster observed the people in the cottage, he learned _____.
1 how to play piano
2 how to cook
3 how to read
4 how to dance

_____ c To make a female companion for the monster, Frankenstein went to _____.
1 the Orkneys
2 Mont Blanc
3 Ingolstadt
4 Russia

_____ d Who did the monster kill after Frankenstein's marriage?
1 William.
2 Elizabeth.
3 Mr Waldman.
4 Walton.

3 Read the sentences below. Complete the second sentence so it means the same as the first. Use no more than three words.

[a] My main interest was the living body.

I was mainly _____ the living body.

[b] But when I saw the monster, horror and disgust filled my heart.

I was horrified _____ when I saw the monster.

[c] Every day I feared the monster would do some new evil act.

Every day I was worried the monster would do _____ bad.

[d] I will not create an an evil companion for you.

I refuse _____ an evil companion for you.

PROJECT WORK

Divide the class into three groups. Each group chooses a topic from below to research, preparing a presentation for the rest of the class, as a poster, on the Interactive White Board, or as a talk.

GOTHICS AND ROMANTICS

Frankenstein is an example of a Gothic horror novel. Find out more about other Gothic novels and poems of the same time, *Dracula* for example. Find out also about the Romantic movement, which included the English poets Percy Shelley and Lord Byron. What did the Romantics believe? When did they write and what were their most famous works?

FILM AND TV VERSIONS

Find out which were the most important film and TV adaptations and when they were made. Did the film makers change or add to Mary Shelley's story? Find out as much information as you can, including which actors appeared in the films and which locations were used.

TRAVELS IN THE 18TH CENTURY

Research the places where Frankenstein travels in the story. Find information and pictures of places like the North Pole, Lake Geneva and Mont Blanc. Draw Frankenstein's route on a map. Find out about the importance of travel and the Grand Tour in the 18th century. Find out more about Mary Shelley's travels around Europe.

作者簡介

瑪麗·雪萊生於 1797 年，本名瑪麗·歌德溫，英國作家，作品涵括小說、短篇故事、戲劇和旅遊雜記。《科學怪人》於 1818 年匿名出版，當年她二十歲，這是她最為人熟知的作品。她嫁給英國浪漫主義詩人柏西·比西·雪萊。

瑪麗的母親在她僅僅出生十一天之後就過世。四年後，父親娶了鄰居瑪麗·珍·克萊蒙為妻。1814 年，瑪麗·歌德溫愛上當時已有家室的雪萊。兩人和她同父異母的姊姊克萊兒·克萊蒙一同前往法國，環遊歐洲。在雪萊的第一任妻子哈莉葉自殺後，於 1816 年與雪萊結婚。

1816 年，瑪麗、柏西和詩人拜倫等一夥朋友在瑞士日內瓦附近避暑。這一群朋友比賽寫恐怖小說，瑪麗便開始寫起了《科學怪人》。1818 年，雪萊一家人離開英國，前往義大利。他們育有兩子，但都夭折。瑪麗最後生下兒子柏西。

但在 1822 年，丈夫過世，他的小船在暴雨中沉沒，因而滅頂。一年之後，瑪麗返回英國。她當起作家，賺取稿費養活她的兒子。她在世的最後十年，都在病痛中度過，最後死於腦瘤，得年 53 歲。

在 1970 年代之前，瑪麗最為人熟知的作品是《科學怪人》。近年來，她的另一部歷史小說《瓦爾佩爾加》（1823）和旅遊雜記《漫步德國與義大利》（1844），被挖掘問世。

本書簡介

《科學怪人》這部小說，描寫一位年輕的科學學生在科學實驗中創造出了一個生物。這是一部偉大的恐怖小說，但也探討了哲學上的一些觀念，以及人類是否有權「扮演上帝」的議題。這是一本極早期的科幻小說典範。

1816 年夏天，瑪麗·雪萊與丈夫柏西·雪萊，連同拜倫和其他友人一同前往日內瓦旅行。由於天候惡劣，大夥無法外出活動，便待在屋內消磨時間。他們閱讀恐怖小說，接著比賽寫恐怖小說。瑪麗想像一個科學家創造了一個生物，卻反被他所創造的「東西」所嚇到的故事，她的想像最後成為了《科學怪人》的故事。

這本小說除了告誡執迷的危險，也談到了孤獨的問題。這個怪物之所以會行徑失控，是由於外表被排斥，而非本性惡劣。在故事中，他幾次展現了他良善的一面。

小說出版後，有批評家評說「恐怖又噁心」，但其他評論家驚訝的是這本小說竟出自女性之手。然而，《科學怪人》非常暢銷，並於 1823 年搬上舞台劇，從此廣為人知。之後，也有多部電影、電視劇和戲劇改編或源自於這本小說。

序幕

P.13

17XX 年，探險家羅伯特·華頓從英國前往俄羅斯，尋找橫越北極進入太平洋的航道。他想成為第一個搭船前往那裡的人。他是讀數學、科學和醫學的，經歷過許多危險的航程。華頓常寫信給住在英國的姊姊，跟她說自己的旅行見聞。其中有一封信很特別，提到了一段奇異而充滿恐怖、痛苦和苦惱的駭人奇怪故事。

P.14

17XX 年八月五日

親愛的姊姊：

這個星期我們遭遇了一段奇遇。我們的船被冰原和濃霧所包圍。濃霧散去後，我們看見遠方出現一個身形非常壯碩的男子，坐在幾條狗拉的雪橇上，朝另一頭遠去。這真是不可思議，因為我們距離陸地和文明世界有幾百公里遠。

隔天破冰後，水手們準備啟航時，看見另一名男子出現在一塊浮冰上！男子渾身凍僵、瘦削，而且疲憊不堪。我們立刻邀請他登上我們的船，但他說他想先知道我們的船要開往哪裡。我們告訴他，我們要前往北極，他才同意加入我們。

他說，他正在追捕一個逃跑的人。我跟他說，我們前一天看到一個身材高大的男子。他聽了很激動，還問了我一堆問題。接著，他跟我說了他的事，算是要警告我和所有的人。所以，親愛的姊姊，我現在就把男子告訴我的事，說給你聽。

第一章

P. 15

我叫做維克多‧法蘭根斯坦，是日內瓦人。我的父親是一位富有的商人，在瑞士很有名氣。他娶了一個家境貧窮的女子為妻，年紀比他年輕許多。他們經常在歐洲旅行，而我出生於那不勒斯。

我的母親經常造訪窮苦人家，接濟他們。有一回，在科莫湖附近，她拜訪一個養育了五個飢餓孩子的家庭。其中有一個小女孩，她身材細瘦，長相清秀，和其他孩子的外表不同。當母親問起小女孩的事，這戶人家的女主人說，小女孩是孤兒，她的雙親生前是有錢的貴族。

我的父母同意收養她，將她帶回自己的家裡扶養長大。這個女孩名叫伊莉莎白，她成了我最好的朋友。她喜歡讀詩，親近自然，而我喜歡探究自然界的

祕密和運作的法則。我七歲時，我的么弟出生，父母不再四處遊歷，他們返回日內瓦，落腳在鎮上的一棟房子，還有一棟鄉村小屋緊鄰湖邊。

P. 17

我的另一個摯友叫亨利‧克勒弗，他是商人之子。只要是和中世紀有關的東西，亨利都很著迷，尤其是亞瑟王和圓桌武士。他常要我們扮成中古世紀的騎士。亨利對於美德和英雄特別感興趣，希望長大後也能成為這樣的人。我們的童年過得很快樂。伊莉莎白善良又溫順，她都帶著微笑和一對漂亮的眼睛看著我們玩。

儘管我有一個無憂無慮的快樂童年，我總是渴望能夠學習其他的事物。我想知道天文與地理蘊藏的奧祕。十三歲時，我無意間發現了科尼里烏斯‧阿格里帕的一部著作，這給我開啟了一個嶄新的世界，我感到非常幸福。

阿格里帕
‧利用網路，尋找更多科尼里烏斯‧阿格里帕的資料，將找到的資料與小組討論。

P. 18

父親要我別把時間浪費在閱讀這種書上面，但沒有跟我說為什麼。所以我繼續以一個孩子的觀點獨自閱讀，雖然我對書中的內容並不完全了解，心中仍帶著好奇的求知欲。

這個情況持續了幾年，直到我看到

雷擊發出的閃電把一棵樹燒得精光。當時，家中一位博學的客人將他對電學和電流的所有知識理論，描述給我們聽。這些主題對我來說新奇又有趣，我便將多年來研究的阿格里帕擱置一邊，立刻全心投入研讀數學和科學。

這或許是我的「守護天使」最後一次保護我免於遭到雷擊，而這道雷擊當時已等著要落在我身上。

第二章

P.19

十七歲時，我遭遇了人生的第一個不幸。伊莉莎白得了猩紅熱，由母親照顧。不久，伊莉莎白的病好了，母親卻染上惡毒的疾病，撒手人寰。她在病榻前，說她希望伊莉莎白可以跟我成婚。

之後，我離開了日內瓦，進入英格爾史塔德大學就讀。我頭一回感覺到孤獨。我的人生一直以來與世隔絕，在我啟程之際，一想到嶄新的知識正等著我，內心不免感到愉悅。

我立刻前往拜訪首席教授。機會——或者應該說「毀滅天使」如今控制了我的人生——帶領我先去會見自然哲學的教授克倫培先生。當他得知我鑽研像科尼里烏斯·阿格里帕這樣的古老作家時，他說我完全在浪費我的時間。接著，他列了一串近年出版的書籍，要我添購並閱讀。不論如何，我決定不去聽他的課，因為克倫培先生不但長得醜，而且身材矮胖，聲音難聽。

P.20

老師

- 你的老師長得什麼樣子？
- 告訴你的朋友，你覺得最差勁的老師是誰，還有原因。
- 你認為老師很和善或是很會教書是否重要？小組討論。

P.21

我後來去見了化學教授華德曼先生。他和克倫培先生截然不同：他的年紀約莫五十歲，容貌慈祥，聲音悅耳。他在課程開始時，簡述了化學史以及近年的發展。他接著提到科學的近況，並解釋許多基本詞彙。

他也做了幾個初步的實驗，之後他開口說道：「古代教授科學這門課程的老師，總是承諾學生會發生不可思議的事，卻什麼也沒發生。現代教授很少做

出類似的承諾，卻著實創造出奇蹟。他們獲得嶄新且近乎無限的力量。」

他說這番話時，我感覺到真的活了起來。他的話語碰觸我的內心深處，不久，我的心裡便充斥了一個想法：儘管前人已經完成這麼多的成就，而我，法蘭根斯坦，我會成就更多。我將會尋找嶄新的方式，探究未知的力量，將萬物最深層的奧祕向世人展現。

我決心回到古老的研究，全心投入我自認為我有所天賦的科學。我前往造訪華德曼先生，把我早年的研究告訴他。他說，我也應該研讀自然哲學和數學，學習化學家必備的知識。他還列出書單，要我去購買。這真是難忘的一天，這一天決定了我未來的命運。

第三章

P. 22

此後，我只專注在自然哲學和化學科目上。我勤加研讀，上課聽講。我進步神速，其他的同學和教授都感到吃驚。經過兩年持續不斷研讀和實驗，我改良了一些化學儀器，在大學裡頗受敬重。

後來，我所達到的成就，讓英格爾史塔德大學無法再幫助我的發展。我正

打算返回日內瓦，但這時候發生了一件事，讓我又多留了一些時日。

我的主要興趣是人體。生命從何而來？這是大哉問。我鑽研生理學和解剖學，日日夜夜地待在墓地，觀察人類軀體的腐壞過程。經過日以繼夜的投入，我發掘了生命的起因，更重要的是，我能夠讓沒有生命的物質活起來。

P. 23

我思索該如何利用這種驚人的力量。雖然我能夠賦予生命，但要替一副軀體備齊肌肉和血管，是何等艱困的事。

最後，我決定自己創造人類。這個人的身高兩公尺半，體型壯碩，因為打造嬌小的軀體困難重重。花費幾個月時間收集與備妥材料後，我開始著手進行。

我的內心充滿了熱忱和精力。我打破了生與死的謎團，替黑暗的世界帶來光芒。我要打造一個將我視為造物者的嶄新物種。希望自己有一天能夠起死回生。我不眠不休工作，變得瘦削與蒼白。我到墓地收集骨頭，解剖室和屠宰場提供了所需的人體其他部分。我在頂樓的獨立房間工作。有時，我恨透了自己做的事，但是瘋狂的熱情使我繼續下去。

P. 24

這段期間，我完全沒有跟家人聯繫。我沒有留意到季節的更迭，也不與其他同學往來。我睡得不好，經常感到心悸和恐懼，但內心依然埋藏著決心，宛如一盞明亮的燈帶領我前進。

目的

- 你是否有過目的或計畫，讓你在完成前不曾闔眼？例如閱讀一本書、學校的報告、製作影片，或是打電玩？你的感覺如何？把想法告訴朋友。

第四章

P. 25

最後，十一月的一個漆黑夜裡，我完成了我的工作。我整理好賦予躺在腳邊生物生命的各項儀器，就著燭光，看著這個生物張開眼睛，他呼吸沉重，四肢迅速抽搐。

我該如何描述當我看見自己投注無數心血與工作，所創造出這個災禍時的心情？我替他挑選俊美的五官，俊美？老天！泛黃的皮膚底下，覆蓋了肌肉和血管，烏黑的頭髮散發出光澤。牙齒是珍珠白。但是這些俊美的五官，卻與他水汪汪的眼睛、皺摺的臉龐和兩片直直的黑色嘴唇，形成一個駭人的對比。

將近兩年的時間，我辛勤工作，但如今作品完成了，夢想的美好也隨之消失。我的內心充滿了恐懼與反感。

我衝出房門，躺在自己的床上，想要忘掉創造出來的生物。我在夜裡驚醒，月亮發出昏黃的光線，我卻看見自己創造出的可怕怪物。他站在我的床邊，看著我。他張開嘴，發出聲音，我卻不明白他在說什麼，而且還露齒笑著。我從

他身邊衝出去，整個晚上待在外頭，緊張地不停來回踱步。

P. 27

六點鐘一到，我衝到潮濕、陰暗的街道，每到一個轉角，就害怕跟那個怪物碰個正著。我奔跑著，渾身被滂沱大雨淋濕。我來到外地來的馬車停靠的旅館。一輛瑞士來的驛馬車停了下來，令我吃驚的是，亨利·克勒弗步出馬車。

「親愛的法蘭根斯坦！真高興一下車就見到你！」他說。

我很高興見到童年時期的玩伴克勒弗。他將我帶進對父親和伊莉莎白的回憶，以及對我來說很重要的家庭景象。一時之間，我忘卻了自己的恐懼與不幸。這是許多個月以來，我頭一回感覺到平靜與快樂。我們一塊走回公寓，一路上聽著亨利談到我們的朋友和家人的

事。

他繼續往下說：「但是，親愛的法蘭根斯坦，你看起來瘦削又蒼白，好像幾天沒睡。」

「你說的沒錯，我最近在忙著一個計畫，不允許自己休息。不過，現在計畫已經完成，我終於自由了。」我回答。

我們一塊走著，我渾身顫抖。我想到那個怪物可能還待在我的公寓，擔心亨利會見到他。所以當我看見公寓裡空無一人，很高興。我們一塊享用早餐，但是我根本坐不住。我從椅子上跳起來，拍著手，大聲笑著。

「維克多！別這樣笑！你病得真重呀！發生了什麼事？」亨利大喊。

P. 28

「別問！」我大喊著，雙手遮住眼睛，「救救我，救救我！」

我開始罹患了神經性熱病，一連幾個月沒有離開過房間，亨利是唯一照顧我的人。在這段生病期間，這個怪物總是出現在我的眼前，我發瘋似地談論著他。我以極其緩慢的速度恢復了健康，隔年春天才康復。

「親愛的克勒弗，你真的對我非常照顧。」一天早上，我對他說：「除了念書之外，整個冬天都在這個房間裡照顧我。我要如何回報你？」

「趕快恢復健康，然後寫封信給你的父親和伊莉莎白，他們會很高興收到你的親筆信。」他說。

「當然，我一定會寫信給他們。」我說。

「既然你心情很好，你可能會想讀伊莉莎白寫給你的信吧？這封信寄來已經一

段時間了。」他回答。

伊莉莎白在信中說，她很高興聽到我恢復健康的消息，希望我可以盡快回信。她告訴我，父親無恙，我的弟弟厄尼現在已經十六歲，想要從軍。小弟威廉現在長得又高又迷人，有著一對藍眼睛和一頭捲髮。她在信末說到，他們很感激亨利把我照顧得這麼好。

P. 29

之後，我將亨利引介給大學裡的幾位教授。華德曼先生和克倫培先生都大大讚揚了我的研究，令我感到很難為情。但為了遺忘這一切所帶給我的緊張不安，還有我創造出的那個怪物，我放棄了先前的研究，轉而跟隨亨利研究東方語言。

我本來打算秋天回日內瓦，但是我不想讓克勒弗獨自留在異地。接著，冬天下起了雪，大雪覆蓋了地面的路。隔年五月，亨利跟我在英格爾史塔德地區旅行，我們花了兩個星期探索這個地區。那真是一段快樂的時光，我們一路上話題也不斷。返回英格爾史塔德大學後，我恢復了健康，精神飽滿。

第五章

P. 30

返回公寓之後，我收到父親寄來了這封信：

親愛的維克多：

你大概在等我的信，以便決定返家的日期。然而，恐怕你這趟返家之行不會愉快。威廉死了！維克多，他遭到謀殺！

上個星期四，伊莉莎白、你的兩個弟弟和我，我們前往普蘭帕蘭散步。我們比平常多待了些時間，但等我們返家後，伊莉莎白和我找不到厄尼和威廉。他們在玩捉迷藏。厄尼回來後，說他找不到威廉。我們一直找到半夜才回家，原以為他可能已經到家，卻不見他的蹤影。我們帶著火把，繼續外出尋找他。

約莫清晨五點鐘左右，我發現了摯愛的兒子，他的頸部留下雙手的勒痕。

伊莉莎白不斷自責，因為她讓威廉帶著價值不菲的項鍊，項鍊的墜子上還有母親的小型畫像，而項鍊不翼而飛了。顯然這是凶手行兇的動機。

快回家吧，幫我們撫平內心深處的傷痛與失落。

你摯愛的父親
阿爾方斯‧法蘭根斯坦

我的雙眼擒滿淚水，我放下信紙，示意克勒弗讀信。

他讀完信後，說道：「我不知道該說些什麼，我的朋友。失去親人的不幸，難以彌補。你打算怎麼做？」

「我要立刻返回日內瓦。」

P. 33

一路上，我的心情十分複雜：我難過小弟的死，卻又開心能在相隔近六年後再見到父親、伊莉莎白和厄尼。當我終於見到日內瓦湖，還有環繞四周的群山，我不禁喜極而泣。

我打算先前往威廉喪生的普蘭帕蘭。我搭船越過湖泊，抵達岸邊時，天空開始下起大雷雨，雨勢持續增強，閃電照亮整個湖面，我提起精神大聲喊道：「威廉，親愛的天使！這是你的喪禮，你的輓歌！」

突然間，一道閃電照亮一個從一些樹叢間鑽出的身影。我不會看錯，他正是我賦予生命的可怕怪物！他怎麼會到這裡來？難道是他殺害我的弟弟？我開始對這個念頭深信不疑。他不斷朝我的方向走來，等到下一道閃電出現，我看見他輕易登上附近山壁的陡峭岩石上。

我不敢移動身體，大雨持續下著。離他被賦予生命至今，已經兩年了。難道我創造出一個喜歡殺人、給人帶來痛苦的怪物？我整個晚上待在那裡，渾身濕透，十分憂慮。那個怪物難道要摧毀我摯愛的一切？

P. 34

到了五點鐘，我才抵達父親的房子，

因此逕自返回書房休憩。過了一些時候，弟弟厄尼走了進來。

「歡迎，親愛的維克多，真希望你是三個月前回來，當時我們過得很幸福。我希望你能夠安慰我們的父親，還要伊莉莎白別再為威廉的死而自責。」他說。

我的雙眼充滿淚水，厄尼又說了些伊莉莎白的狀況：「她自責是她造成弟弟的死，但是凶手很快就被找到……」

「找到凶手！」我大喊。「老天！這怎麼可能？誰能追捕到他？我也看見他了，他昨天晚上還能自由行動！」

「我不懂你在說什麼，」我的弟弟很吃驚，他答道：「找到凶手，卻讓我們更加不幸。我們的僕人賈絲婷‧莫瑞茲，她對我們家人一向親切慈愛，誰會想到她會突然犯下這椿駭人的罪行？」

厄尼解釋說，找到威廉屍體的那天早上，賈絲婷就開始臥病在床好幾天了。其中一名僕人檢視謀殺當晚她所穿的衣服，在衣服的口袋裡找到那條有母親畫像的項鍊。僕人將項鍊交給治安官，賈絲婷被拘捕，並遭到控告。她不知所措的模樣，讓每個人都堅信她犯下這件殺人案。

P.35

「你們都搞錯了，我知道誰是凶手。賈絲婷是無辜的。」我說。

過了一會兒，等父親進來書房後，厄尼大聲說：「父親，維克多說他知道是誰殺害了可憐的威廉。」

「我們也都知道，真遺憾那個我們摯愛與信任的人，竟以這種方式報答我們。」父親說。

「賈絲婷是無辜的。」我說。

「如果她是無辜的，那我們今天就會弄個明白。她今天將接受審判，還她自由。」父親回答。

第六章

P.36

隔天早上，我們前往法庭。證人作出幾項不利於賈絲婷的指控。謀殺當晚，她外出一整夜。之後在天亮時，她在屍體的附近被人發現。她被問道她在那裡做什麼時，又一臉困惑。她大約在早上八點返回住處，說她去找威廉。見到威廉的屍體時，她陷入劇烈的歇斯底里，臥病在床好幾天。那條有畫像的項鍊，是一個僕人在她的衣服口袋裡找到的。

接著，賈絲婷開始替自己辯護。謀殺案當晚，她待在姨母家，伊莉莎白允許她去的。當她返家時，得知威廉失蹤的事，於是外出尋找他的下落。她外出好幾個鐘頭，結果日內瓦城門關上後，她回不了家，所以就待在熟識人家的穀倉裡過夜，沒有驚動主人。隔天早上，她再度外出尋找威廉的下落。如果她在屍體陳屍處的附近出現，那也只是碰巧。而她一臉困惑的模樣，是因為沒有睡好和憂心威廉的安危的緣故。然而，她對項鍊一事，無法交代。

P. 37

之後伊莉莎白開口說：「我和賈絲婷同住在一個屋簷下已有七年之久，她在法蘭根斯坦夫人臨終前，對她悉心照料。她對威廉也是愛護有加。對於被視為主要證據的那條項鍊，我也很樂意送給她。我相信賈絲婷絕對是清白的。」

然而，群眾希望找出這樁駭人謀殺案的兇手，治安官也就此將可憐的賈絲婷定罪。隔天早上，他們告訴我，賈絲婷坦承犯案。我們之後前往監獄探視她。她說，只有認罪，才能洗清她的罪惡，她已經準備受死。

我現在覺得自己才是真正的殺人兇手。

P. 38

賈絲婷死後，我看著這個曾經過得很快樂的一家人。大家都因為威廉和賈絲婷的死，深陷在不幸的崩潰中。這一切都是我一手造成的。我夜不成眠，我做了可怕的事。儘管起初出發點是好意——想對人類做出貢獻，但是我摧毀了一切。我無法帶著喜悅之情回首自己的成就，也無法帶著希望前去尋找嶄新的發現，我只感到後悔、恐懼、絕望和罪惡。

後悔
- 你認為維克多‧法蘭根斯坦會有這樣的感覺對嗎？為什麼？小組討論。

第七章

P. 39

我們後來搬到位於湖邊的房子。我經常在夜裡搭乘小船，在湖上度過幾個小時。我想要將自己投入平靜的湖裡，讓湖水永遠淹沒我的不幸。但是一想到伊莉莎白，我便停止這個念頭。我是如此愛著她，而她已經受了這麼多的苦。

每一天，我都害怕這個惡魔會犯下某件新的罪行。我感覺得到，他並不打算結束。我真希望可以除掉自己不假思索創造出來的怪物。我想要復仇的欲望以及對他的仇恨，充滿我的全身與心思。我想要替威廉和賈絲婷的死討回公道。

有時，處在這樣的情緒折磨中，我需要活動身體，並改變環境。所以在八月中旬，我前往夏慕尼山附近的阿爾卑

斯谷地，展開一段旅行。阿爾卑斯山的天氣和煦宜人，景緻壯闊。大自然的奇觀，令我的身心感覺到舒展。然而不久後，恐懼和絕望會再度向我襲來。最後，抵達夏慕尼後，我感到身心俱疲，當天晚上便沉沉睡去。

P. 41

隔天早上，天空降下滂沱大雨，群山被厚重的雲層覆蓋，但我還是出發前往攀登蒙坦弗特山。山徑狹小難以攀登，不過到了中午，我已經登上山頂。這時，吹來一道風，將雲層吹走，我朝冰河的方向走去，越過冰河。

我現在見到了白朗峰，冰河環繞著冰峰的景觀，真是壯闊。

就在我看著這片景緻時，突然看見一個體型壯碩的男子，正以超人類的速度朝我的方向來。我立刻認出來，他正是我創造出來的怪物。我的內心充滿憤怒與恐懼，決定跟他奮力一搏。

「惡魔！你竟敢靠近我？你難道不怕我會復仇嗎？」我大喊。

「我正等著你這麼做。人們厭惡醜陋的東西，我比他們任何人都醜。但你是我的創造者，你卻想要除掉我？你竟敢如此玩弄生命？你對我盡該盡的責任，我就會對你和全人類盡我該盡的義務。如果你同意我的條件，我會離你和其他人遠遠的。你如果不答應我的要求，我就要殺掉、毀掉你所有在世的朋友。」他說。

「怪物！惡魔！你竟責怪我創造了你。好，你到這裡來，讓我了結你這條如此草率所創造出來的生命。」我尖聲叫喊道。

我朝著他的方向撲過去，他卻輕易跳開說：「請聽我說，我已經受夠了折磨。我是你創造出來的生命，如果你願意彌補你對我的虧欠，我會對你服從溫馴。噢，法蘭根斯坦，你不要對別人和善仁慈，卻只對我毫不留情。俯拾皆是的幸福，竟都與我無緣。我原本是仁慈又善良，但悲慘的命運讓我成了怪物。讓我幸福，我就會變得和善。」

P. 42

「走開！我不會相信你的話。我們是敵人，快走開，不然我們就決一死戰。」我大喊。

「我骨子裡是個善良的人，但是我很孤單。如果你都仇恨我，那我還能期待誰？世人都討厭我，那我怎能不去怨恨

所有的人？而你，可以改變這一點。跟
我到我藏身的穀倉，聽聽我的經歷，再
對我作最後的裁斷。你有能力拯救我。
你可以決定我是否要有一個美好的人
生，或是成為你們人類的惡魔，成為毀
滅你自己的那個原因。聽聽我怎麼說，
法蘭根斯坦！」他說。

　　我一方面出於好奇，一方面對這個怪
物感到虧欠，於是便跟隨他越過冰河。
不久，我們就一塊坐在他藏身附近的火
堆旁，他開始講起他的遭遇。

聆聽

- 你覺得在評斷一個人之前，先聽聽
  他的經歷，是否重要？為什麼？
- 你能不能回想曾經有過對他人妄加
  評斷，最後才發現與事實有出入？
  你發現事實的真相後，內心作何感
  想？把想法告訴你的朋友。

第八章

P. 43

　　怪物於是娓娓道來：
　　「起初，我對一切都感到困惑。我躲
在英格爾史塔德附近的樹林裡生活。我
逐漸學會辨認鳥類、昆蟲、植物和樹木
的名稱。我曾發現一個人類所留下的火
堆，所以我學會讓自己在夜裡取暖。我
飢腸轆轆，便找食物果腹。我發現一間
小穀倉，裡面住的老人正在做早餐。他
一見到我，大聲尖叫後，拔腿就跑。我

吃了他的早餐，接著倒臥在床睡著了。
　　「我睡到中午才起床，繼續往前走。
日落時分，我來到一個村落。這地方似
乎很不錯，有穀倉、小木屋和寬敞的屋
舍，許多屋子的窗台上放了牛奶跟起
士。我進到其中一間比較好的房子裡，
但是孩子們見到我時尖叫不已，一名女
子還暈了過去。全部的村民都來了，有
的人拔腿狂奔，有的人攻擊我。我便離
開了。

P. 44

　　「最後，我在一個離群索居的小木屋旁
發現一棟小屋。房子陳設簡單而乾燥。
我也能夠從牆壁的縫隙望出去，還可以
從一道縫隙鑽進小木屋裡。沒多久，來
了一位年輕的女子，有一個年輕男子來
和她會面後，然後兩人一塊走進小木
屋。我看見屋內有一個愁眉不展的老
人。女子正在做各種雜事，接著她給老
人帶來一把吉他，老人開始彈奏起來，
女子一邊唱和著。這個畫面很美好。稍
後，年輕男子帶回來柴火、一條麵包和
起士。女子煮了從花園裡摘下的一些
菜，然後他們便吃了起來。入夜之後，

一家人便進入夢鄉。

「我想著我所看見的景象，還有人類溫和的舉止。我想要加入他們，但決定先安靜待在原地，觀察並了解他們。我看著他們做事情，也留意到年輕男子和女子帶著敬愛之心來對待老人。不過，有時候他們會聚在一起哭泣。我不知道箇中原因。

「後來，我才知道他們生活很窮苦，常常吃不飽。我之前有時會偷走他們的食物，但是之後就在樹林裡找東西果腹。我也對他們伸出援手。我在夜裡會替他們砍柴，因為年輕男子在白天的許多時間裡都在尋找生火的木柴。起初，他們感到很驚訝，但接著他們花了幾天時間修復木屋，整理花園。

P. 46

「這樣觀察與聆聽他們，我學會了許多

基本的詞彙，還有他們三人的名字：父親；兄長、兒子或菲力克斯；妹妹或阿嘉莎。

「隨著冬天的到來，我學會更多他們的話語。他們的父親失明，所以兒子有時會朗讀給他聽。我想要認識善良慈愛的一家人，但我知道自己得學會好好使用他們的語言。我羨慕他們姣好的面貌，而我知道自己是個怪物，因為我在池中見過自己的倒影。

「我白天的生活，差不多一成不變。早上，我觀察他們的作息；中午小憩一番後，下午和傍晚繼續觀察他們。如果當晚夜裡無雲，我會前往樹林找尋食物，並替他們砍些木柴。春天到來時，我感覺自己的內心充滿了喜悅。

「有一天，一位女子來到小木屋。菲力克斯見到她之後，悲傷一掃而空，他們的生活也出現了重大的改變。她見了男子的父親和妹妹，但是她不懂他們所說的語言，他們也不懂她說的話。他們開始教她語言，我更加小心追蹤他們的一言一行。女子叫做莎菲，她和我的語言都進步很快。我也跟她一樣學會閱讀，透過菲力克斯教她讀的書，我學會了歷史和社會。

P. 47

「然而，我也了解到，我比低下階層的人類地位更低賤。沒有人像我一樣，我是個人人避之唯恐不及的怪物嗎？阿嘉莎和莎菲的溫柔話語，老人和菲力克斯的對話，都不是對我說的。他們談論家人、朋友和孩子，但我的家人在哪裡？我的過去空白一片。我生來就是這樣的

身高和體型，從未見過自己的同類。我
究竟是什麼？」

過去

• 你能想像自己沒有過去嗎？你會有
什麼感覺？向朋友描述你的過去。

第九章

P. 48

怪物繼續往下說：

「經過一些時候，我才明白，雖然我
跟人類有著相似之處，但是其中有一點
截然不同：我不依賴任何人生存，也沒
有任何親友。當我不在了以後，不會有
人思念我。我的外貌醜陋，令人無法直
視，而且身形巨大。這意味著什麼？我
是誰？我是什麼？我從哪裡來？

「現在我學會了閱讀，蒐集了一些你所
寫的一些文章。你在創造我之前的四個
月撰寫過日記，鉅細靡遺描述了一切。
內容顯示你對自己所做的事感到恐懼。
我愈讀，愈感到病態。我納悶你為何創
造一個連自己都厭惡且避之唯恐不及的

恐怖怪物。但是我的鄰居很善良，我想
跟他們做朋友，跟他們一起快樂過生
活。我見過他們對門前的窮人從不吝於
施捨，覺得他們不會出於恐懼而拒絕幫
助我。

P. 49

「我思索著要如何向他們介紹我自己。
我決定等失明的老人獨自一人的時候，
再進去小木屋。我知道自己醜陋的外
表，是人們懼怕我的主要原因。我覺得
如果讓老人站在我這邊的話，年輕一輩
的鄰居或許就能夠容忍我。一個溫暖的
冬天午後，莎菲、阿嘉莎和菲力克斯前
往田野間散步一段時間，我看到機不可
失，於是敲敲小木屋的門。

『是誰？』老人問：『請進。』

我走進入屋內，說道：『抱歉，我是個
旅人，想找個地方歇腳。能否讓我坐在
火堆旁幾分鐘？』

『進來吧。我的眼睛看不見，我的孩子
們不在家，所以沒辦法替你準備食物。
你是法國人嗎？』老人說。

P. 50

『不是，不過我在一個法國家庭長大。
現在希望能夠得到一些摯愛友人的庇

護，我希望他們願意幫我。但是他們沒見過我，我很害怕，因為如果我沒辦法跟他們成為朋友，我在這世上將永遠孤單一人。』我回答。

『這真是令人難過。你要是跟我說說你的事，或許我能幫上忙。』他回答。

『謝謝你！』我開心地說：『我欣然接受你慷慨的幫助，希望在你的協助之下，他們不會把我趕走。』

『我能夠知道這些朋友的名字，以及他們住在哪裡嗎？』他問。

我握住他的手說：『你跟你的家人就是我的朋友。別留下我一人獨自受苦。』

『老天！你是誰？』老人大喊。

「就在此時，小木屋的門開啟了，菲力克斯、莎菲和阿嘉莎走進屋內。我很難描述他們見到我的時候，臉上那種驚恐的表情。阿嘉莎昏厥了過去，莎菲衝出小屋外，菲力克斯衝上前來，將他的父親跟我拉開，把我推倒在地，拿起木棍用力對我猛打。我的心一沉，感到不適。我內心充滿痛苦與憂慮。我離開小木屋，打算返回住處，永遠不再被人類看見。

P. 51

「噢，我該死的創造者！我的處境如此悽慘。等到夜晚降臨，我進入樹林間遊走，發出嚎叫。沒有任何人會可憐我，或是幫助我。我向人類宣戰，也無法原諒讓我面對這樣可怕苦境的創造者。夜深之後，我返回住處。

「之後，菲力克斯和一名男子出現在屋內，我聽著他們的交談。

『你知道你們得支付三個月房租，還有花園內的收成嗎？』男子問。

『等你聽完我跟你說的事後，我們不會繼續住在這裡。請你收回小木屋，讓我盡快離開這個地方。』菲力克斯說。

「我再也沒見到這家人，我跟這個世界的唯一連結消失了。我的內心充滿報復與仇恨之情。我先摧毀花園內的一切，接著放火燒了小木屋。

怪物
• 你對這個怪物感到憤怒還是同情？

P. 52

「我決定接著下來去找你，你是我唯一可以請求憐憫的人。我從你的日記中得知，你住在日內瓦。但是我要如何找到路？既然不能向人類探路，太陽成了我唯一的指引。這段旅程很漫長，我受盡了折磨。我啟程時，已是秋末，我只能在夜裡趕路，以避人耳目。途中，又下雨，又降雪，寬闊的河水結成了冰，大地寒冷，一片荒蕪。等到早春之際，我才來到了瑞士。

「有一天，我在林間漫步，但我沒有往常一樣找地方躲藏與休息，因為天氣和煦，我感到很舒暢。我來到一條又湍急又深的溪河邊，這時我聽到了人聲，於是趕緊躲到一棵樹後面。

「有一個小女孩在河邊奔跑嬉戲，結果腳底一滑落入溪水中。我費了好大一番力氣爬下來，救起了她。她已經昏過去了，就在我試圖幫她時，跟她一塊

來的男子出現了。他衝了過來，從我手中將女孩抱走後，便跑開了。我也不知道為什麼，就跟了過去，而他卻轉過身來，朝我身上開了一槍。

「這就是我所得到的回報！我拯救了人類的性命，現在卻陷入痛苦之中。我恨透了所有的人類，決定無論如何都要展開報復。我待在林子裡幾個星期，肩膀的傷口才逐漸復原。

P. 54

「然後我前往日內瓦，躲在附近的田野間，決定要怎麼對付你。

「我躲在附近時，看見一個長相俊俏的孩子。我突然想到天真的孩子應該不怕我。我如果帶走他，我可以教育他，把他當成朋友，我在這世上就不會再感到孤單。所以男孩經過時，我抓住了他。

他一見到我，就發出尖叫，遮住自己的雙眼。我將他的手從臉上移開。

『我不想傷害你，聽我說。』我說。

『放開我！你這個醜陋的怪物，想要吃掉我。放我走，不然我就跟我爸爸說。』他大喊道。

P. 55

『你不會再見到你爸爸了，你得跟我走。』我說。

『放我走！我的父親很有聲望，他是法蘭根斯坦先生。他會懲罰你！』他大喊。

『法蘭根斯坦！你是敵人的家人！那你將成為第一個受害者！』我大叫。

「我用雙手掐住他的脖子，不一會兒，他就倒臥在我的腳邊。當我望著他時，感覺到一絲的勝利感。我知道男孩的死，將帶給敵人絕望。之後我注意到他

戴著一條綴有美麗女子畫像的項鍊，於是便將項鍊取走。

「尋找藏匿處時，我來到一間穀倉，卻驚訝見到一名年輕女子睡在穀倉裡。我望著她，心想絕對不可能會有女人愛我。她可以頂替我殺害男孩的罪名而受罰。所以我把那條有著畫像的項鍊，放進她的口袋裡。

P. 56

「我在這地方逗留了一陣子，最後前往附近的山巒，打算永遠待在這裡。我孤苦無依，命運悲慘。人類將永遠與我沒有任何牽連，但是，一個跟我一樣醜陋和可怕的女子，就不會拒絕我。我的同伴得是個跟我同類的人。你要替我創造一個。」

他講完後，盯著我看。我只感覺到威廉的死所帶給我的憤怒。

「我不答應，我為什麼要另外創造一個像你一樣的怪物，讓你們兩個人在世上幹壞事？走開！」我說。

「你錯了，我之所以邪惡，是因為我很不幸。每個人都討厭我，所以我為什麼要去同情對我毫無憐憫之情的人類？如果我無法讓人類愛我，那我就讓他們怕我。我復仇的對象，主要是針對你。當心點，要不然我會毀掉你。」他回答。

愛

• 你認為愛可以阻止人們做出邪惡的事嗎？小組討論。

P. 57

我思索他說的話，我了解到，他如果是幸福的，也許就不會再給人類製造問題。

「如果我同意你的要求，只要我替你創造出一個女性同類，你發誓你會立刻永遠離開歐洲。」我說。

「我發誓，」他大聲咆哮道：「如果你同意我的要求，你就永遠不會再見到我。現在快點幹活去。我會仔細觀察你的進展，等你準備好，我就會出現。」

他迅速離開下山。我立刻動身返回日內瓦。眼前的整個情勢，讓我悶悶不樂。當我再度見到家人時，幾乎開心不起來。為了解救他們，我得執行這項可怕的任務。

任務

• 維克多・法蘭根斯坦得怎麼做？
• 這項任務為什麼可怕？

第十章

P. 58

幾個星期過去，我卻無法展開我的工作。我害怕那個怪物出現，厭惡自己承諾的事。這一天，父親說他要找我談。

「維克多，我一直期待你跟伊莉莎白可以結婚。你們向來很親近，我在想，你現在對她的感覺，是否不只是表妹和朋友？」

「別擔心，父親，我跟伊莉莎白終究會結婚的。」我回答。

「這真是好消息，你有意盡快成婚嗎？」他回答。

我不禁想起我對怪物的承諾。我怎麼能夠在實現可怕的諾言之前結婚，並過著正常的生活？我得偷偷找地方躲起來，完成這個可怕的差事。這些感覺幫助我回答父親的問題。我告訴他，我得先返回英國一年。我沒有向他解釋確切的原因。我的父親欣然同意，他希望這個改變可以幫助我的身體和精神完全復原。

P. 59

九月，我啟身前往英國。我擔心怪物會趁我離開時傷害我的家人，但也相信他會跟我前往英國，所以家人應該是安全無虞。亨利·克勒弗陪同我前往英國。我們沿著萊茵河而下，行經鹿特丹，再搭船前往倫敦。

在倫敦時，我拜訪了一位重要的自然哲學家，為這一樁令人不悅的工作蒐集新的資料。亨利樂於前往印度著手蒐集關於如何組織的資料，而我蒐羅所需的

材料。有個朋友邀我們前往蘇格蘭的伯斯，我們一路上行程緩慢。

我仍然遲遲未動工，所以感到不安，不知道怪物可能會做出什麼事情來。我讓克勒弗留在伯斯和朋友在一起，而我前往奧克尼斯北部一座偏遠的小島，待在一間小木屋內完成我的任務。隨著時間過去，我發現自己愈來愈難完成這個駭人的差事。而每當我抬頭時，總是心想怪物會出現在眼前。

第十一章

P. 60

一天夜裡，我琢磨自己正在幹的好事。我不知道這個女怪物可能會是什麼模樣。我第一個創造出的怪物答應會離開歐洲，但是她的女伴就不一定了，她

113

説不定會比他還要邪惡。如果他們繁衍後代，我不就在這個世上創造出一個種族生物了嗎？

這時，我突然一個抬頭，竟看見怪物正站在外頭，他盯著我看，露齒而笑。他跟蹤我，等著我完成作品。但在他的臉上，我只見得到邪惡。我想到，我答應他的事，是何等瘋狂。我害怕得發抖，於是在他面前將創造的作品扯個粉碎。他絕望地發出可怕的咆哮，接著消失不見。

我返回自己的房間，聽見腳步聲和開門的聲響，我知道怪物來找我了。

「你毀了你的作品，你竟敢破壞你的承諾？我一直在等你實現諾言，現在你毀了我的希望。」他説。

P. 62

「走開！我的確打破了承諾，我絕對不會再創造另一個像你一樣的惡魔。」我大喊。

「還記得我擁有的能力，我能讓你陷入絕境。你是我的創造者，但我是你的主人。服從吧！」他説。

「你不能逼迫我做邪惡的事，我不能幫你創造一個邪惡的伴侶。」我大聲咆哮：「走開！」

「你會後悔的，我現在一心只想要復仇。」怪物大聲呼喊：「你記住，我會在你的新婚之夜現身。」

「怪物！在你殺掉我之前，先確保你自己的安危吧。」我尖聲喊道。

他快步離開。之後，我看到他乘船離開。接著，我想到他的威脅：「我會在你的新婚之夜現身。」所以我得先發制人。

兩天之後，我收到一封克勒弗寄來的信，信中要我跟他一起返回倫敦，完成他在印度的事業。我回到實驗室，收拾我的一切儀器。我將所有恐怖的混亂東西放進籃子裡，並塞滿石頭。當天稍晚，我划著船出海，把籃子從船沿扔進海裡。

海面平靜，夜裡有月光，我待在船上睡著了。等我醒來，海風和海浪變強。我無法控制住船，便任由風帶著船走。我望著天空中的雲層迅速飄移，接著望著海面，心想自己將葬身大海。過了很久之後，我喜出望外地看見了陸地。天氣此時平靜多了，我沿著海岸停靠在一個小港口。我把船繫在岸邊時，人們很快便聚集過來。

P. 63

我聽見他們用英文交談，我開口說：「抱歉，請問這裡是哪裡？」

「你等一下就知道啦。」一名男子說。

「你怎麼回答得這麼不客氣？」我問。

「厭惡壞人，這是愛爾蘭的傳統。你要跟我去找柯爾文先生，解釋清楚。」他回答。

「誰是柯爾文先生？我為什麼要向他解釋？」我問。

「柯爾文先生是治安官，昨天夜裡這裡有人遭到謀殺，你要交代清楚。」他說。

他的回答讓我很吃驚。儘管我又累又餓，我還是跟他去了一趟，準備證明我的清白。

愛爾蘭

• 維克多‧法蘭根斯坦現在來到愛爾蘭，查閱地圖，或是上網跟隨他從奧克尼島海域出發，前往愛爾蘭北邊海岸的旅程。

第十二章

P. 64

我被帶到治安官的面前，他傳喚證人。一名水手說明道，前一天晚上，他們在離小鎮有一段距離時，因為強風暴雨，便返回陸地。他們發現一具年輕男子的屍體，屍體仍有餘溫，是被人勒斃的。聽到這裡，我渾身發顫，想起了我的弟弟威廉。

其他證人看到一艘跟我一樣的船，上面坐著一個人，在案發附近出沒。之後，我被帶去指認屍體。當我看見亨利‧克勒弗的屍體時，想像我內心是何等感受！

「亨利，我的所作所為害死了人，也害死了你？我已經毀了兩個人。但是你，克勒弗，我的朋友，我的幫手……」我哭喊著。

我暈厥了過去，被帶離房間。我臥病在床，躺了兩個月之久，差點沒命，嘴裡胡亂地喃喃念著被殺害的威廉、賈絲婷，以及如今也遭殺害的克勒弗。

這一天，我醒來時，發現自己被囚禁在監獄。柯爾文先生偶爾會來探望我，來看看我的情況。這天，他告訴我，我父親來探監。

P. 65

父親告訴我，他和伊莉莎白、厄尼都很好。父親首度前來探視我之後，我的病情逐漸好轉，但是心情卻更加沮喪。亨利遭到殺害的駭人畫面，不斷在我眼前出現。我希望為自己犯下的罪受到懲罰，好結束我的不幸。

在監獄囚禁了三個月之後，法庭才聽見我的證詞。大陪審團決定對我不予以起訴，因為證據顯示，友人的屍體被發現時，我仍待在奧克尼。很快地，我就獲釋出獄。

我想要盡快返回日內瓦，這樣我才能看好我摯愛的三個人。我想藉此尋找怪物的藏匿地點，他如果膽敢再來找我，我就會要了他的命。

我理所當然經常想起他對我說過的話，「我將會在你的新婚之夜現身」。這件事很可能發生，他會在我的大喜之日夜裡，把我殺掉。他對我的壓制將會結束，我最後將獲得自由。

P. 66

不過，這不代表他在此之前就會按兵不動。克勒弗的死，證明了這一點。

返回日內瓦後，大半的時間裡，我心情低落，只有伊莉莎白可以撫慰我。我們決定在十天後成婚。婚禮在張羅著，而我準備著對付怪物的攻擊，我的身上一直配帶著手槍和刀子。

但日子一天天地過去，大喜之日愈來愈近了，我開始希望一切可能不會有事。

婚禮結束之後，父親的住處辦了一個隆重的宴會，而我們倆人搭船前往艾維昂，準備在那裡過夜。

第十三章

P. 67

我們在八點時上岸，沿著岸邊走了一小段距離，享受著夜光，然後返回下榻的旅館。這時，天空降下大雷雨，我的恐懼再度襲來。我緊握著身上帶的手槍，決定和怪物作殊死一戰。

一想到伊莉莎白要目睹我決一死戰，那對她是何其可怕之事。於是，我吩咐她先上床睡覺。我繼續在走廊上走來走去，尋找敵人的下落。

突然間，我聽到一聲淒厲的尖叫聲。我衝回房間，伊莉莎白已經斷氣了！兇手把她拋在床上，我昏厥了過去，過些時候才清醒過來。

之後我站起身來，撫摸伊莉莎白冰冷的屍體，看見她的脖子留有怪物雙手的勒痕。接著當我望向窗外時，見到怪物就站在那裡，他咧嘴笑，用手指著我的亡妻。

我衝向窗邊，開了槍。他往湖邊快

步奔去，往湖裡縱身一跳。人們聽見槍響，紛紛追了出來。我們追逐兇手的下落，但一無斬獲。

P.68

我立刻返回日內瓦，憂心父親和厄尼的安危。我回到父親的住處，他們都還安然無恙。然而，父親聽見伊莉莎白的噩耗，感到震驚。幾天後，便因傷心欲絕而過世。

我跟日內瓦的治安官陳述了我的事，我說，我知道是誰摧毀了我的家庭，請他搜捕兇手。他難以置信地聽我講述，感到很駭人。最後，他說他很樂意去搜尋怪物，不過因為怪物似乎擁有超越人類的力氣，他也不能保證能否抓到怪物。他說，我應該先做好心理準備。

我告訴他，我想要復仇，如果他無法幫上忙，那我會自己動手。

如今，我恨透了日內瓦，於是帶著母親遺留的金錢和珠寶，離開這裡。我展開一連串的旅程，唯有斷氣，才會停止。我四處奔波，直到敵人喪命，我不會停下腳步。

P.70

離開之前，我來到威廉、伊莉莎白和父親的墓地。我站在他們的墓前，大聲說：「我承諾，在找到這個可怕怪物復仇之前，我都會好好活著。我現在所感受到的悲慘滋味，我也要讓他嚐一嚐。」

我聽到一陣狂妄的邪惡笑聲傳來，接著是憤恨的聲音，說道：

「我很高興聽到你這個可憐的傢伙決定

117

過冰海，沒有前往陸地的方向。他們相信，他很快就會沒命，不是凍死，就是落入裂開的冰河而死。

P.72

我將雪橇換成容易在冰海前進的雪橇，備足許多食物，接著便離開陸地。有時，冰山阻擋了我的去路，其他時候我聽見冰融的聲音，只是下一秒又再度結冰。我經常怕自己在斷氣前追捕不到敵人，但是經過一番掙扎越過一些冰山後，我看到他在遠方的身影，再度燃起希望。我跟他相距不遠，再過兩天，我將離他不到兩公里的距離。

追隨

· 沿著地圖，追隨法蘭根斯坦和怪物的旅程。

就在我感覺到自己快追捕到他時，浮冰開始裂開。不久，我跟敵人之間將隔著一道寬闊大海。我陷入絕望，直到看見你們的船。我將自己所在的浮冰「小島」，向著你們的方向靠近。我想跟你要一艘船，前往追捕怪物，而你們正好要前往北方，救了我一命。我對此感到喜悅，因為我的任務還沒有完成。

P.73

如果我在死前沒有追捕到他，而你卻找到了他，華頓，答應我，你會替我殺了他，替威廉、賈絲婷、克勒弗、伊莉莎白和我父親的死復仇。還有我的死。

活下去。」

我就著月光，看到他以超越人類的速度，迅速逃離。

我沿著隆河，來到地中海，越過俄羅斯，一路追捕。我經常處在寒冷、飢餓、疲憊不堪的狀態。怪物有時候會留下記號給我，像是一個指引方向的箭頭，或是一段訊息：「你活著，我就擁有力量。跟我走，我要前往結冰的北方，你將感受到寒冷與冰雪的淒涼，而我感覺不到。在我們決一死戰之前，你將經歷無數艱困與不幸的時光。」

我買下雪橇和狗隊，以便趕上他。在我來到冰海時，我只落後他一天的路程。

他前一天晚上抵達這裡，取走村民的雪橇、狗群和過冬的食物。他打算越

華頓

- 誰是華頓?翻到 13 頁查看。

曲終

P. 74

17XX 年八月底,羅伯特·華頓寫完了維克多·法蘭根斯坦的事跡。他接著寫信給姊姊,說了接下來幾個星期發生的事。

17XX 年八月二十六日

親愛的姊姊:

讀完了這個駭人的驚悚奇怪事件,你是否跟我一樣,嚇得血液都凝結了呢?

我目前被浮冰包圍,浮冰很可能隨時會撞破船。天氣極為酷寒,有幾名水手也都已經喪命。有幾名水手要我能夠允諾,等到船隻可以自由航行的時候,我們可以往南行。

但是,法蘭根斯坦質問他們,都大老遠來到這裡了,為什麼要返航。他稱讚他們的勇氣,還說等他們找到越過冰層前往太平洋的航道,他們將成為英雄,而這正是這趟探險的目的。他懇求大夥繼續旅程。

我請大家考慮法蘭根斯坦所說的事,但也對他們說,他們如果決定不依從,我就不會繼續朝北方前進。

P. 75

17XX 年九月九日

冰層開始鬆動。此時,法蘭根斯坦非常虛弱。

17XX 年九月十一日

　　船隻已經完全脫離冰層的包圍，前往南方的水道向我們敞開。水手們見到眼前這一幕，莫不興奮叫好。法蘭根斯坦清醒過來，問大夥為了什麼原因歡呼。

　　「因為他們不久就能夠返回英國。」我回答。

　　「你們真的要返航？」他問。

　　「恐怕是這樣，他們不願意繼續航行，我不會帶領他們去他們不想去的險境。」我回答。

P. 76

　　「隨你想要怎麼做，華頓，但我不會跟你們一道返航。我的目的很清楚，我一定要追捕我的敵人。」他說。

　　我前去找船上的醫生。他說法蘭根斯坦只剩下幾個鐘頭的生命。過了一會兒，他把我叫到他的身邊，說道：「華頓，我還是希望我的敵人可以喪命。我創造了他，應該親手把他殺掉，但我失敗了。請答應我，如果你找到他，你會殺死他。我不久人世了，而他仍然在世，可以幹壞事，這讓我很憂心。」

　　幾分鐘後，法蘭根斯坦便斷氣了。我走出船艙，呼吸一些新鮮空氣。現在是午夜，船隻正往英國的方向前去。突然，我聽見船艙傳來可怕的聲響。我走下階梯，打開艙門。正如法蘭根斯坦所描述的，站在我面前的，是一個巨大而醜陋的傢伙。

　　當我進入船艙時，他正打算從窗戶跳出去。我從未見過任何比他那張臉還要令人作嘔的東西。

　　怪物看看我，然後指向法蘭根斯坦的方向。

　　「他也是我的受害者，隨著他的死亡，一切都結束了。噢，法蘭根斯坦，在我藉由摧毀你全部所愛的人來摧毀你之後，我現在可以請求你的原諒嗎？但他身體冰冷，不會答覆我。」他說。

　　「你的報復太過火了，如今，法蘭根斯坦已經死了，這都是拜你所賜。」我說。

P. 78

　　「你以為我樂在其中嗎？」怪物問道，「我返回瑞士時，很同情法蘭根斯坦，我恨透了自己。但當我發現他竟敢期望得到我永遠都得不到的幸福

「你似乎很清楚我的事。我怨恨，難道不是因為菲力克斯把我趕走，或是因為被我救起的孩子父親反倒射了我一槍？他們都是善良的人，只有我不是。這一切對我來說，是這麼不公平，讓我感到非常氣憤。

「我的確很殘忍，我殺害年輕與無辜的人，他們從未傷害過我，我讓我的創造者活在不幸之中。而現在，他倒臥在這裡斷氣了，面色蒼白，渾身冰冷。

P. 79

時，我感到嫉妒。之後我想要對自己遭遇的所有不幸，展開報復，這成了我唯一一心一意想要做的事。現在，一切都結束了，他是我最後一個受害者！」

「怪物！這並非憐憫之情，你大聲咆哮，是因為你的受害者已死，不再受你的力量掌控。」我大喊。

「不是這樣的，」他打斷我的話，說道：「我曾經夢想人們會接受我本來的模樣，而不要被我的外表影響。犯罪，使我比最低等的人還要不如，但就算最惡劣的罪犯，也有家人和朋友。而我在這個世上，連一個朋友也沒有，孤伶伶一個人。

「你恨我，但是你對我的恨，比不上我對自己的恨。別擔心，我不會再繼續作惡，我的任務差不多完成了。我會離開你的船，找一塊浮冰和一些樹枝，升起喪禮之火。我會在火堆中將自己燒死，這麼一來，就沒有任何人能夠找到我，再創造一個跟我一樣的人。唯有在死亡中，我才能夠安息。再見！」

怪物說完這段話之後，便從船艙的窗戶跳往下方的浮冰。不久，便消失在無盡的黑暗中。

121

ANSWER KEY

Before Reading

Pages 8-9

1 a) T b) F c) T d) F e) T

2 a) 1 b) 5 c) 3 d) 6 e) 2 f) 4

3
a) One dark November night.
b) Yellow.
c) No.
d) Shiny black hair and pearly white teeth.
e) His yellow skin only just covered the muscles and veins beneath. He had watery eyes, lined face and straight black lips.
f) 1. instruments
   2. lined
   3. emotions
   4. selected
g) monster

Pages 10-11

5 a) 2 b) 3 c) 1

6
a) dissecting room
b) slaughterhouse
c) cemetery

7
a) students, professors
b) philosophy, physiology, anatomy, chemistry
c) veins, muscles
d) tombs
e) decay

8 a) 2 b) 3 c) 3 d) 3 e) 3

After Reading

Page 81

9 a) F b) T c) F d) F e) T
f) T g) F h) T i) F j) F
k) T l) T m) T n) F

Page 82

10 a) science
b) night
c) monster
d) letter
e) deaths
f) hate
g) revenge

11
a) To study decay.
b) It was difficult to make the body parts small.
c) To make the monster a female companion.

12
a) The necklace, which William was wearing and was later found with Justine.
b) The cottage, which the monster set fire to after the blind man and his family left.
c) Frankenstein's journal, which the monster read.

Page 83

13 a) Walton
b) Elizabeth
c) Mr Krempe and Mr Waldman
d) William
e) monster
f) Justine Moritz
g) old blind man

14 a

Page 84

15 a

17
a) He wants to be part of a family.
b) He decides that he wants to make people fear him because they do not love him and he wants revenge.
c) He now only wants to take revenge on Frankenstein.
d) He feels bad about what he has done and is going to kill himself.

Page 85

18 a) Frankenstein
b) monster
c) Frankenstein
d) monster

19 a) 4 b) 6 c) 1 d) 2 e) 9
f) 5 g) 3 h) 7 i) 10 j) 12
k) 11 l) 8

23
(*University*) mathematics, philosophy, professor, chemistry, experiments, lectures, science
(*Emotions*) regret, horror, joy, despair, disgust, anguish
(*Death*) graves, funeral, deathbed, cemetery, decay, murderer, tombs

24 a) lectures
b) chemistry
c) tombs, decay
d) cemetery
e) joy

25 a) had worked, had disappeared
b) had begun, had destroyed
c) had created
d) had confessed
e) had seen

26 a) 5 b) 6 c) 2 d) 3 e) 1 f) 4

27
a) I told them they were all wrong and that I knew the murderer, and that Justine was innocent.
b) I shouted at him to make him go away and said I would not listen to him as we were enemies.
c) I promised that I would live until I had taken revenge on this horrible monster.
d) He swore that if I agreed I would never see him again, and told me to go and start my work.

Test

Page 91

1 a) 1 b) 1 c) 2 d) 1

Page 92

2 a) 3 b) 3 c) 1 d) 2

Page 93

3
a) interested in
b) and disgusted
c) something
d) to create

國家圖書館出版品預行編目資料

科學怪人 / Mary Shelley 著；David A. Hill
改寫；盧相如 譯. 一初版. 一[臺北市]：寂天
文化, 2016.9 面；公分. 中英對照

ISBN 978-986-318-493-5 (平裝附光碟片)
　　1. 英語　2. 讀本

805.18　　　　　　　　　　　105014997

原著 _ Mary Shelley
改寫 _ David A. Hill
譯者 _ 盧相如
校對 _ 陳慧莉
製程管理 _ 洪巧玲
出版者 _ 寂天文化事業股份有限公司
電話 _ +886-2-2365-9739
傳真 _ +886-2-2365-9835
網址 _ www.icosmos.com.tw
讀者服務 _ onlineservice@icosmos.com.tw
出版日期 _ 2016年9月 初版一刷（250101）
郵撥帳號 _ 1998620-0 寂天文化事業股份有限公司